T0095644

Other novels by the same author:

Shaya

Alternating Worlds

Workshop of the Second Self

The Kicker of St. John's Wood

THE EMBRACER

Gary Wolf

iUniverse, Inc.
New York   Bloomington

The Embracer

iUniverse books may be ordered through booksellers or by contacting:

iUniverse
1663 Liberty Drive
Bloomington, IN 47403
www.iuniverse.com
1-800-Authors (1-800-288-4677)

Because of the dynamic nature of the Internet, any Web addresses or links contained in this
book may have changed since publication and may no longer be valid. The views expressed
in this work are solely those of the author and do not necessarily reflect the views of the
publisher, and the publisher hereby disclaims any responsibility for them.

ISBN: 978-1-4401-7424-7 (sc)
ISBN: 978-1-4401-7425-4 (ebk)

Printed in the United States of America

iUniverse rev. date: 9/29/2009

The fool folds his hands and eats his own flesh.

—Ecclesiastes 4:5

PART ONE

CHAPTER ONE

▼

From his tenth-floor cubicle overlooking the atrium, Harris surveyed the activity on the courtyard below. The morning rush hour was in full swing, and people were darting every which way in a frantic scramble to their cubicles. He released a sigh of satisfaction, knowing that they were about to join him in a task of incalculable importance. It involved, without question, one of the greatest surges of technological development in the history of mankind. He felt comforted to be nestled within this mass of brainpower, all of it laboring in the service of one common goal.

Harris took a deep breath, rotated toward the computer, and applied himself to the grand enterprise of designing the ultimate cyberbiological commodity. Following the breakthrough by Wong and Hutchinson-Mendoza the week before, his entire department had been buzzing with excitement. They were not alone. The most talented individuals throughout the TransTech world were engaged in a frenzied race to capitalize on the latest discovery. It was only a matter of days—or even hours—until someone, somewhere, solved the last mystery standing in the way of megapulse mind modulation; or, as it was called in the industry, the Triple M.

As a Class 5 cyberengineer, Harris had been assigned some fairly complex programming duties in the project. He felt, however, that these duties were far below his capability, and that his knowledge of the field as well as his overall intellectual acumen were being underutilized.

He believed that this was due, in large part, to the jealousy and vindictiveness of his manager, Bettina Mandrake, who sought to prevent his promotion within the InterFun Software Company.

No doubt, thought Harris, the pattern would continue at that morning's weekly status meeting in Mandrake's office. Nothing beneficial ever seemed to transpire in those sessions. When Harris first joined InterFun some eight years previously, he took seriously her lectures about their joint future. But as time went on, he was increasingly disturbed by her efforts to limit his professional development. Matters were not improved by his abhorrence of her skin-flattening procedure, nor by the presence of the bizarre crustacean that lived in a tank located a mere two feet from Harris's left shoulder when he sat in his usual spot.

Presenting himself at her office that morning at the appointed hour, he noticed that the creature was quietly munching on a piece of raw hamburger. No sooner did he sit down than Mandrake opened with the usual chatter. Harris's mind wandered, as did his eyes, until they settled near the top of his superior's bosom, framed as it was by an oversized neon plasticase. The skin was pale white, with a clammy texture, and stretched beyond repair by the recent flattening procedure. He glanced again at the crustacean.

"Are you paying attention?" inquired Mandrake.

"I was just admiring the new filtration system in the tank," he replied, snapping out of the reverie. He was no longer surprised by his readiness to utter such disinformation. It had become a critical element of his strategy for survival.

"Tell me something, Harris," said Mandrake. Do you think that InterFun has a chance to grab the Triple M?"

"I don't see why not," he answered, without emotion.

"I have an important piece of news for you," she announced. "We have been given the opportunity to play a more visible role in the Triple M. But it all depends on one thing: Are you capable of taking on some additional—shall we say special—responsibilities for the project?"

"Absolutely," said Harris, solemnly.

"Good. Tomorrow I want you to meet with some people from R&D. I think they can explain what's going on much better than me."

Harris's eyes tensed as a craving for cephanil juice enveloped his nervous system. It was the vagueness of the matter that was afflicting him. The possibility of a trap loomed large. This would not be the first time that someone of his rank was sacrificed at the Triple M altar. On the other hand, he reasoned, it might really be a cunning plan on the part of Mandrake for their mutual benefit.

"Sounds good," he said, sluggishly.

Mandrake indicated her contentment with a fat smile, though her eyes betrayed a slight suspicion. "I'll set it up then. We have begun."

After returning to his desk, Harris stared into the monitor, groping for inspiration. What little he had was temporarily frozen by the meeting with Mandrake. She had a way of paralyzing his creative energy. He popped some bunga nuts into his mouth, sat back in the ergosnap chair, and looked around at the environment where he had spent most of his waking hours for eight long years.

His office, and indeed the entire facility, was designed and furnished in what Harris called "imitation big-time." From a distance, everything glistened in steely tones. But up close, there was no doubt as to the cheapness of the merchandise. The ubiquitous paneling, for example. From a distance, one was certain that a rich, dark wood graced the lower third or so of the office walls. But upon closer inspection, there was no doubt that it was fake, not even plywood or some other variant of a former tree. Harris noted that over the previous several months, the paneling had begun to peel, and the color was fading in spots into a yellowish-brown hue.

At mid afternoon, he began to formulate a notion of the entertainment to be pursued that evening. A weekend, at the very least, was required for a trip to the Coast, so as usual it boiled down to a choice between Clickville and the Cyclops Bar. There were no other options to speak of in that part of the WestTech zone. Harris chuckled under his breath as a vision passed through his mind of himself at age ninety in Clickville, hobbling with a cane from arcade to arcade. Was this the inexorable path of his life? Maybe he would suddenly become rich and retire to the Coast. It was at this point in his recurring daydream that he experienced a severe melancholy.

He briefly considered contacting his friend Lincoln, who worked in the legal department. A few weeks earlier, the two had made grandiose plans to engage in some brain fulfillment down at the Coast. At the last minute, however, Lincoln opted for a triple cerebral plunge, which predictably left him in a stupor, unable to travel. In Harris's eyes, Lincoln was becoming an unreliable partner for leisure activity.

To describe Lincoln as a friend is somewhat of an overstatement. He was simply a coworker who shared a common interest; namely, highly developed methods of distraction. This they did once or twice per month, and that sufficed. No other joint activities were pursued. There was rarely a topic of conversation beyond the matter at hand, except for an occasional comment regarding work.

Harris arrived at the Clickville amphidrome a bit early that evening and took a seat in the west arena, about three-quarters of the way up. From there he had a commanding view of the festivities, and, as a result of his fastidious calculations, the best acoustics. He ingested a large quantity of bunga nuts and settled in for the ride.

The show presented that evening was The Frenzy of Canaan. Twelve nearly-identical females, each propelled by a jetpack, dive-bombed from above. They stopped and hovered in the middle of the great space, about level with Harris's vision. Their feline features were starkly illuminated from the light projected upon them from all directions. Each erstwhile lady, in a seemingly uncontrollable whirl, unleashed a stream of defecation upon some cyberwarts on the floor of the arena. Some of the audience, by now driven into an ecstatic delirium, elbowed their way to be directly under the torrent.

It was all over much too fast. As he pulled out of peak state, Harris experienced his customary letdown. He muttered to himself about finding a better amphidrome, and contemplated his options for the remainder of the night. Would he take in the cow-drag? Or perhaps a tour of the smaller Clickville arcades? Instead, beset by the usual angst, he found himself wandering toward the QuickRail train, reconciled to an early night. At least at home, he figured, he could treat himself to a mood hookup.

The stimulation experienced by Harris at Clickville had been significantly greater when he first began attending the spectacles some three years previously. Then, it was all new. Lincoln was credited with introducing the brain-fulfillment park to Harris, who never would have ventured into such an establishment alone. He had been perturbed by the sight of the public defecation. Lincoln, with great patience, explained the underlying principle: The act was symbolic of humanity's drive for liberation, for self-realization. By viewing such a release of tension, such a bursting of societal chains, one would be energized and inspired to pursue psychic exploration and spiritual growth.

These words of wisdom launched Harris into years of satisfaction. Lately, though, the magic had worn off. On occasion he recounted Lincoln's speech, if only to convince himself that he should be enjoying the event more than he actually was.

He stepped onto a standporter that whisked him past the other attractions of Clickville on his way to the QuickRail station. En route, he surveyed the array of diversions that beckoned to the cyberwarts of the WestTech zone. The air for some distance seemed electrically charged from the mixture of haze and artificial light. Looking at the twisted faces of his fellow WestTech warts as they filed into one or another house of amusement, Harris felt an anguish welling up from his gut. He perceived a vague need for an alternative environment, but the sensation fizzled away as his mind returned to its habitual lethargy.

After a short ride on the QuickRail, Harris stepped off at the Los Perdos station and began the half-mile walk to his apartment. As always, he contemplated the urban landscape. All of the buildings in the neighborhood had been erected at about the same time. The construction was hasty, using highly polished but shoddy materials. For example, the facades of most of the buildings were plated with a thin sheet of marble. At first, it lent an attractive sheen to its host structure, and many of the new homeowners bragged about the bargain they had found: an affordable and stylish dwelling. After several years, however, the life span of the cheap adhesive used to fasten the sheets expired, and fragments began to fall. People were killed or injured. By the time Harris arrived, ways had been found to fasten the remaining plates securely in place. But the facades remained pockmarked and distorted, creating an eerie and intimidating effect.

The residential tower in which Harris had been living for almost two years was the epitome of mediocrity, if it even attained that level. Everything was clean and well-maintained, but it was bland in the extreme. The colors were dull and the architecture contained nothing beyond what was necessary for the building to stand. The only exception was the lobby, which had tacky, bluish-gray glass in several spots. Harris considered this embellishment to be gratuitous, as if to say, "look, there really is something here for you worthless warts." Overall, though, he was pleased to be there. It was a significant step up from his previous quarters.

One explanation for the slipshod construction in Los Perdos is the era in which it was built. Numerous cultural conflicts, starting in 2018, had resulted in wars and widespread destruction. This was followed by the Division, the cataclysmic event of the 2020s that led to the separation of the planet into two broad political entities: the TransTech world, and an agglomeration of weak, impoverished regimes known collectively as "outerwart territory." TransTech, in turn, was divided into administrative districts called "zones." One of these was WestTech, which before the Division was an area that included most of California and its neighboring states. In many areas of the WestTech zone, such as Los Perdos, the war damage was particularly severe. Thus the pressing need for quick construction.

The apartment itself offered no surprises. The walls and ceilings were all made from the same smooth, featureless, off-white plaster. The floor looked about the same, only it was made from more durable material. The windows were few and far between.

Upon arrival, Harris washed up and fixed himself a cephanil freeze. Along with bunga nuts, cephanil juice was the workaday drug of the TransTech world. Although producing a powerful narcotic effect, bunga and cephanil allowed the user to function normally. It was as if a person's power of reason and clarity of thought were distilled and set apart, protected from the impact of the substance. Meanwhile, the body and the more spiritually-oriented portions of the brain became thoroughly medicated.

He wandered lazily to the window and peered out. A light drizzle had begun to tap the exterior. From the nineteenth floor, he had a commanding view of the other towers in Los Perdos, which were identical to his own. Harris reflected on his current situation, a regular occurrence at this late hour of the day. He muttered, grumbled, and vowed to do something, and then felt ridiculous at having made the same resolutions as on the previous day.

One perennial item on the list of complaints was his intolerable work arrangement. Harris could no longer avoid the oppressive conclusion that he had reached a dead end at the InterFun Software Company. His progress, he reckoned, was perpetually blocked by the merciless Bettina Mandrake and her allies. He clenched his teeth: How many times would he let them walk all over him? On several occasions he had drawn up elaborate plans for revenge, but when the critical moment arrived, he took no action. Instead, he sank back into his bog of apathy. The frustration was compounded by the knowledge that some of his peers were involved on a daily basis with the cutting edge of cybertechnology.

His analysis of the issue led him to a deeper level. He was convinced that at the root of his life's chronic malaise was his inability to reach a higher state of altered consciousness. He had exhausted virtually every available avenue: cyberbiological products, such as the mood hookup; mass brain-fulfillment spectacles, such as dive-bombing; and a potpourri of group mind-expansion techniques. Granted, there were additional variants in all of these categories, but they were out of reach either financially or physically. If a higher state of altered consciousness could be achieved—so went his reasoning—he would acquire the wherewithal to extract himself from the dead end that he faced.

After arriving at work the next morning, Harris set his face in front of the computer, absorbing the initial news of the workday. In the datapile were instructions from Mandrake for the day's session with Beecely, the head of research and development. They were to discuss the Triple M, starting at 9:15 AM in Theater 14. There was not enough time to properly launch a task, so he spent several minutes watching one of his favorite archived cow-drags.

Feeling unmotivated, Harris set out for Theater 14. The room was used primarily for orientation in advance of a new assignment. Arriving a couple of minutes early, he found himself alone in the dark and colorless space. It resembled a small planetarium, with a collection of computers and other machines in the center, surrounded by several concentric rings of seats. Each seat had its own workstation, with a swiveling personal datapad.

The last time Harris had been in that wing of the InterFun compound was to test a new product. At one time, a great hope for boosting the company's declining market share was LifePulse, a product that could rearrange (virtually, that is) a person's life, for his own gratification. Harris found the entire experience to be fascinating. Seated at a specially-equipped computer, his first chore was to complete a long questionnaire that covered a vast swath of his life experience. Next, he entered an enormous quantity of data, including photographs and documents. He then plunged into the follies of his life, noting all mistakes, regrets, stupid purchases, worthless relationships, and so on. Where relevant, he added the desired alternative result. Finally, he described his dreams, goals, and fantasies.

LifePulse never made it to market. At first, it seemed to function properly: the product generated a hexaflash presentation of the individual's life as it *should have* occurred. It was like watching the fulfillment of one's most exalted ambitions, with all supporting characters behaving as required and all circumstances turning out to be fortuitous. There was a problem, however, with the scenarios concocted by LifePulse. They were at best irreverent, at worst downright insulting. Harris's film, for instance, portrayed him as commander-in-chief of an army, despite the fact that he had not conveyed any information whatsoever to the program on this subject. Such a turn of events was the farthest thing from his mind, and the last outcome he would ever want. Similarly bizarre results were obtained by the other testers.

Presently, he was joined by Beecely and another senior colleague, Lapidarius. Beecely was an affable-looking man in his early fifties. Balding, wearing a respectable but somewhat worn gray suit, he looked the epitome of the nice guy next door. Harris had studied under him at the WestTech Academy, and then worked on his team for a short while after joining InterFun. The two had had a contentious relationship from the outset, and never had a kind word to say about each other. To put it mildly, Beecely would not be Harris's first choice of supervisor for a special assignment.

Following the salutations, Beecely stepped aside to attend to the main computer. Lapidarius, not two-thirds of Harris's height, stood close by, but with his face turned slightly away. Harris could not discern whether he was poised to engage in conversation or was floating off into his own little world. The outer rim of his lips was permanently retracted, producing a pallid, almost cadaver-like effect. This, together with a pair of nervous, twitchy eyes, left the observer with the constant anticipation of speech. Harris felt a certain repulsion from Lapidarius, despite his admiration of the noted cyberscholar. His groundbreaking exploits in cybertechnology were well-known throughout the WestTech zone.

"Harris," said Beecely, "everyone in R&D has heard of your good record."

Harris considered this remark to be nothing but vacuous pandering. It reminded him of his earlier session with Mandrake.

"You're not the loud type," continued Beecely. "But you're solid and dependable. That's why you're here right now."

Harris caught himself gnawing on the left side of his lower lip, and turned away slightly. Beecely pointed to one of the seats. "Just sit down over here and absorb the datastream."

He happily complied, easing his overtaxed body into the seat next to Lapidarius, who was aiming his facial contortion at some point above their heads. The datapad poured forth a short hexaflash presentation on the quest for the Triple M. With no intermission, Beecely rolled into his own remarks concerning "our joint steps forward from this point." He paused to collect his thoughts, and then leaned menacingly over the workstation. "What does all this mean for you, my friend? Put quite simply, it's your golden opportunity to step up to the plate, as they used to say." Then, with a more serious tone, almost in a hush: "You're old enough to remember the *Division*."

At the mention of the word, Harris's spine stiffened.

"Sorry, I know it's something one doesn't mention in polite conversation. But these are extraordinary circumstances."

Harris craved cephanil juice so intensely that his feet were locked against the base of the seat.

"Let me be blunt, Harris. We have made contact with some outerwarts across the Line, in the city of Jeptathia. They may have solved the last mathematical equations needed for completion of the Triple M. This is exactly what Lapidarius and his team have been working on day and night for the last six months. We want you to go there and get the equations."

Harris tried quickly to make sense of the entire affair, but his mind kept wandering to an image of himself frantically dashing into his apartment and wiring up a double cerebral plunge.

"You have been selected for the most delicate of missions," explained Beecely. "You'll be going to a place that doesn't have bunga nuts, or the simplest mood hookup, in order to advance the frontier of cyberbiology. Why, you may ask?"

Harris found himself involuntary leaning toward the datastream emanating from his superior's mouth.

"My dear sir, there are warts out there who have never even heard of cephanil juice, who have never had a cerebral plunging. Do you realize what I am saying? Their minds are untouched since birth."

Harris pondered the sheer vulgarity of such a specimen. Before he had time to work out the permutations, Lapidarius chimed in.

"Yes, their brains are the perfect laboratory," opined the veteran engineer. "There are people out there who can solve complex mathematical problems, purely in their heads, for hours at a time, and all this without a single external stimulus. Incredible."

Beecely leaned back onto the center table across from Harris, and abruptly put an end to the discussion: "I think that's enough for today."

Back at his office, Harris struggled to calm his frazzled body and organize his thoughts. He could not help reliving the scene in Theater 14. Even a hasty cephanil infusion could not ease his discomfort. Eventually, he gathered his wits sufficiently to reflect on the facts of the case. This special assignment by all opinions should be considered a plum. Some of his peers would engage in every manner of piracy to secure such a step-up on the InterFun ladder. Yet he suspected a trap. The setup was too good to be true.

Harris also was dismayed by the prospect of having to exit the TransTech world, if only for a day. It was many years since he had crossed the Line, and that was before the Division. He thought of recent incidents in which cyberwarts had ventured into the wasteland, only to return in a coffin. Of course, they had entered the more remote regions. Jeptathia, Harris reminded himself, was an urban area, with some semblance of order.

He began to settle down. On the computer, he watched another cow-drag, this one being broadcast live from Clickville. The quality of the show was entirely acceptable for a midday interlude, though Harris smirked as he recognized the make and model of the cloned bovine creature, from a low-grade series that was hopelessly inferior.

His thoughts were rudely interrupted by the slantbeam, whose frenzied beeping and flashing begged for attention. He signaled his acknowledgment of a message from Mandrake informing him that he would immediately begin a period of intensive preparation, and then go fetch the equations.

Two solid days of preparation passed without a hitch. A fair amount of time was spent learning about the equations. Harris also was apprised of the particulars of the preliminary agreement with the outerwarts, and of the possible impediments to a swift conclusion of the deal. He was given limited authority to negotiate; in case, for example, a lower than expected number of equations were ready for delivery.

He was briefed about proper behavior in the presence of the outerwarts. They demanded a high level of courtesy and politeness, including some rather meticulous table manners. In fact, etiquette played a large role in their social intercourse. All of this, naturally, was merely a facade meant to dissimulate their real nature: savage, crude, and back-stabbing. But the emissary would be obliged to maintain appearances, and be more cunning then these masters of deception. In Harris's favor was the fact that a successful conclusion of the equation deal was very much in the outerwarts' interest.

He also received instruction on the current state of outerwart territory in general, and Jeptathia in particular. The city was large by their standards, and home to an intellectual and cultural elite, to the extent that such a term was applicable. One thing was certain: Although they were a backward nation—stubbornly refusing in the twenty years since the Division to adopt the Charter of the TransTech world—they did excel in various fields, particularly mathematics. Although their cities were rat-infested dumps, many of them were masters of abstraction. InterFun was about to reap the benefits of the labor performed by these idiot savants.

It would not be the first time that InterFun advanced its agenda in such a fashion. Harris had seen several cases where the company, on the verge of fading into obscurity, revitalized its operations by acquiring the fruits of someone else's brainpower. The deal would always be consummated quietly so that InterFun could take full credit. He recalled the time when the company had poured the greater part of its research and development effort for several months into a device that could sense the approach of certain predetermined individuals. Everything seemed fine in theory and even in design, but the CloakMaker project became bogged down in the testing phase. There were a number of mishaps: a datapad caught fire, a test subject became deaf in one ear when the alarm went haywire, and the sensors at one point were activated by the presence of dogs within two hundred yards. These dilemmas threw InterFun into a quandary. There were delays, and more delays. The outside world was becoming suspicious.

The bug was solved by burying the problem within an academic competition for a group of prodigious outerwart high school students on the other side of the planet. A student named Chang Sun succeeded in debugging the code. Sun received a scholarship to the university of his choice. As it turned out, he decided to defect to the TransTech world, and began a stellar career at the WestTech Academy. Meanwhile, InterFun boasted of its unequalled brain trust, the greatest collection of cyberengineers in all of WestTech. It was only a year later that the public learned of the connection between the student competition and CloakMaker.

By the eve of his departure, Harris had reconciled himself to the necessity of the mission and his role therein. The old cloud of apathy and passivity once again enveloped him. But it was a cloud that would soon be swept from the sky.

Chapter Two

▼

The big day arrived. Harris departed from the InterFun compound in a hypercush, a small high-speed vehicle that ran along a fixed track. The vehicle's navizoom indicated that it would take one hour, twenty-two minutes and thirty seconds to reach the Line.

As he peered out from the vehicle, Harris exhaled a sigh of exasperation. He should be thrilled, said one part of his mind, but instead he was experiencing a rather large wave of apprehension. He failed to see how any good could come of this adventure. If the equations were so important, he figured, why didn't Beecely go get them himself? Something was awry. It smelled as bad as a rotting bunga nut.

The rapidly advancing hypercush crossed the giant WestTech urban mass and continued into the desert. Having no interesting scenery to observe, Harris passed the time reading an article on the latest technological developments in dive-bombing.

When he pulled to within ten miles of the Line, there began to appear dense rows of cube-flats that housed outerwart refugees who had just made it into the WestTech zone. He viewed the scene with trepidation, and reminded himself that just over the Line it was even worse, a squalor that defied the imagination. He felt fortunate to be living in a clean flat in a reasonably spacious environment.

The hypercush arrived at the border station. An armed bodyguard climbed aboard. Mandrake had insisted that all proper security precautions be followed. Harris felt reassured as he exchanged salutations with his new companion.

The hypercush resumed its trajectory. In minutes, they would arrive in Jeptathia; or, more specifically, in the TransTech enclave within the city. These enclaves, found in all major outerwart urban centers, were fully-protected pockets of TransTech sovereignty. They were a part of a system of capitulations set in place at the time of the Division.

Who were they, these people who could perform astounding mental feats with their untouched minds? Harris combed his memory for scraps of data. He wasn't all that young, already fourteen, when the Division occurred. He occasionally recalled events or people from his childhood, vague as it seemed. For instance, he was fairly certain that an uncle of his had lived in Jeptathia. The uncle, rumor had it, perished in the Bombardments, but Harris was never entirely convinced. Of course, if he had survived and continued to live among the outerwarts, he was as good as dead to his nephew. It was widely known, for example, that the city's residents refuse to attend the most common public festivals, such as dive-bombing. One might as well step into the suction vent of a hypercush if that's to be one's fate, reasoned Harris.

The travelers ramped up to the main hypercush port at the TransTech enclave in Jeptathia. The bodyguard opened the jumphatch and stepped out, followed by Harris. As he turned toward the exit, his head involuntarily snapped back from the startling apparition in front of his nose: a tall, broad-shouldered man wearing a dark purple overcoat. Harris could not restrain himself from examining the face. It contained wrinkles—something he had seen only once or twice in recent years, on outerwarts who had defected to WestTech. An ear-to-ear smile, with teeth exposed, threw the cyberengineer into a state of apprehension. He reluctantly shook the stranger's warm hand, and the unlikely threesome proceeded toward the exit.

An automobile was waiting at street level. Harris and the bodyguard stepped inside, rather gingerly, neither of them having traveled in such a contraption for many years. Harris's fretful mood became amplified when they passed through the checkpoint at the limit of the TransTech enclave. The scenery changed dramatically. Jeptathia was as run down and dismal as the popular conception would have it. Poverty oozed from its streets and buildings like sweat from the pores of the skin.

The automobile came to a halt in front of an old and decrepit apartment building. The group got out of the car and walked to the front door. They entered a dimly lit, peeling corridor, where they were joined by another man. Harris wanted to flee, but calmed himself by remembering Beecely's charge: be a diplomat. Get on their good side, get from them what you need, and then get your wart-corpse out of there. Harris managed, not without exertion, to approximate a smiling movement on his face.

Possessed by a morbid curiosity, he suppressed his natural revulsion in order to comprehend these people. The man who just joined them was a most unusual specimen. Harris scrutinized him as one would a bizarre insect. The skin of his face and hands exhibited a light maroon tint, and was marked by a slight exfoliation. His frame was bulky, with ambiguous divisions between torso, head, and limbs. His occasional glances at Harris revealed a reciprocal degree of revulsion.

The outerwart was unable to contain his feelings. Right there in the middle of the corridor, his entire bulk stiffened, and then in a gruff, agitated voice, he exclaimed: "What's the meaning of all this, anyway?" The others were stunned by the unexpected outburst. His arm gestured toward Harris. "We take this cyberwart into our midst, and for what? For his money! What good can come of it?" His face assumed a deeper, more furious maroon.

The outerwart in the purple overcoat indicated to Harris, by a contraction of the eyes and brow, to remain calm. His grand smile returned, albeit frayed by the circumstances. "Perhaps we should discuss such matters in private," he said. He motioned to Harris and the bodyguard to follow him, ignoring his incensed compatriot. The three of them walked through another corridor, more dank than the previous one, and then began to climb a narrow staircase. Several small children, en route to the ground floor, wiggled their way past the ascending legs. The asymmetry of the architectural elements, the dissimilar raw materials, and the hodgepodge of colors all combined to disrupt Harris's depth perception. For a moment he was climbing without feeling that his overall motion was upward. He felt dizzy from the effects of the peculiar environment.

They stepped into an apartment that seemed like it belonged in another world. The furniture was old and elegant. Numerous bookshelves lined the walls, packed with volumes in several languages. A distinguished-looking mahogany grandfather clock graced the far corner of the room. The complete unfamiliarity of the scene caused Harris's discomfort to rise another notch. A light sweat broke out on his face and neck.

After they were seated, the outerwart asked Harris whether he would like something to drink. He tried to recall Beecely's rules of etiquette, to determine whether there had been any guidelines for such a situation. Remembering none, he asked for some water. "I need it for my medicine" he blurted, as his trembling hand extracted a tube of cephanil juice from his pocket.

The outerwart excused himself to step into an adjoining room. He returned with a canter of water, a glass, and a bowl. Harris froze with amazement—it was a bowl of bunga nuts, and grade AA, as far as he could tell.

The host could not contain a light chuckle as he viewed his guest. "I was told that you might like these." Needless to say, he would not dream of offering his guest one of the expensive cigarettes in his desk drawer, knowing full well that smoking tobacco was a punishable offense throughout the TransTech world.

Harris could find no words, but maintained a pleasant facial expression. He scooped up a fistful of the enticing nuts and ferried them to his mouth in the manner of a gorilla. He was mildly ashamed of his hasty behavior. But the high-grade bunga soon worked its magic, and he quickly entered a state of exaggerated self-confidence alongside a general muscular soothing. He washed down the bunga nuts with a mouthful of cephanil juice, and settled back into the antique wingchair.

The outerwart neither drank nor ate. He carefully removed a large, leather-bound book from one of the shelves and slowly thumbed through the pages before finding the one he was seeking. His arms supported the back of the book, seeming to surround it in a protective bubble. His intense concentration led Harris to believe that the old tome contained material related to the Triple M equations, though the pages seemed musty and worn. When the host noticed that Harris had been soothed, he just as carefully replaced the book, sat down, and resumed his calm, curious look.

After a further exchange of pleasantries—Harris adhering at every word to the Beecely rules—the outerwart opened a small drawer under the bookshelves and removed a small, silver-blue synchbox. "All the equations you desire are here," he said, in a soft voice.

Harris followed the procedure he had so carefully rehearsed: Initial examination of the synchbox; reiteration of the price and method of payment; and review of guaranties of secrecy and anonymity. The only thing that remained would be for him to decrypt and verify the identification codes. For this purpose, a special room, with full cyber capabilities, had been prepared for him in a hotel back at the TransTech enclave. There he could check the codes, contact InterFun for final approval, and execute the electronic transfer of funds.

Within an hour of reaching his hotel room, the deal had been consummated. The outerwart said goodbye and promptly returned to his automobile. After releasing the bodyguard, Harris walked to the hypercush port, adjacent to the hotel.

While waiting for the technician to prepare the vehicle, he felt a surge of pride at having smoothly executed the deal. Mandrake had informed him during the final approval call that he would receive a bonus of three months salary after the equations were processed successfully by Lapidarius and his team. Harris pondered the options made possible by the bounty: Would he pursue brain fulfillment for a solid week at the Coast? Or perhaps purchase season tickets to the Clickville amphidrome? A smirk of self-satisfaction danced across his lips.

The hypercush ramped up to its berth. Harris flashed his palm at the sidescope, and turned his shoulders slightly in anticipation of the opening of the jumphatch. But he had to abruptly halt his movement—the jumphatch did not budge. The sidescope showed no signs of life. Harris froze, his brain struggling to comprehend the incomprehensible reality. On rare occasion, a hypercush would grumble or screech. Total paralysis, however, was unheard of. He gathered his wits and surveyed the scene. The entire station was bathed in an orange glow emanating from a set of emergency lights. All vehicles and monitors were inoperative. The other travelers, though clearly annoyed, did not seem alarmed. He approached a man who was about to leave the port.

"Yup, it's another retrocharge," explained the thin, pale cyberwart. "Second in a month."

Harris, his voice noticeably stressed, poured forth his incredulity, noting that there had not been a retrocharge in WestTech for at least ten years.

"My dear person," said the information source, after exhaling a light condescending snort. "If you haven't noticed it yet, this is not WestTech."

Harris's eyes darted from side to side, like a person who realizes he has just been robbed. This was greeted by a burst of laughter from the other traveler. "Listen, I'm going back to the hotel. No reason to wait here. Good luck." He turned his heels and joined the others, who were apparently headed for the same destination.

There was no other option than to merge into the human stream. About a dozen travelers, quietly resigned to the disruption of their plans, slowly made the trek to the hotel complex. At the reception desk, Harris reserved a room, and then made his way to the bar. From the chatter around him, he learned that the hotel was isolated. For the sixth time in two months, the enclave's umbilical cord—TransTech power and communication lines—was cut off, though the Jeptathia grid still could be tapped for immediate necessities. Restoration of the link would take between two to three days, if past experience were a guide. This eventuality had been omitted from Beecely's otherwise exhaustive training program.

Harris peered around the bar. The apparent normality of the scene put him at ease. This was a meeting point, a crossroads of the TransTech world. About two-thirds of the patrons were roughly of Harris's ilk, alongside an assortment of service personnel and ambitious outerwarts who managed to obtain security clearance into the enclave. Everyone seemed to peaceably coexist, as potentially antagonistic types often do when they find themselves together on neutral ground.

A well-polished cyberwart, looking to be in his early to mid forties, perched himself at Harris's right flank. He ordered an expensive triple hot swiffer which, when served, induced a raised eyebrow from Harris. The cyberwart reciprocated with a nod as he raised the potent brew to his lips. After absorbing the first wave of ecstatic tingle, he addressed himself to the InterFun engineer. "I suppose you're stuck here like me.

What brings you to this nasty corner of the globe?" Although he spoke like a WestTecher, there was a variation to his persona that indicated a different origin.

"I'm a courier," said Harris. "I was sent to the hotel to pick up a document belonging to one of the higher-ups in my company. They didn't trust the various delivery services, so they asked for a volunteer who would cross the Line in exchange for a bonus."

The polished cyberwart's expression remained calm, but his mouth was tense. With his head tilted down slightly, he looked up and said, "I know who you are, Harris, and I know why you're here."

The effect upon Harris's anatomy was immediate. A weakness pervaded his body. He locked his vision on a glass of water at the edge of the bar, as if a remedy would magically appear there. He feared a neuronomy, even worse than the one he had endured years earlier after being accused of plagiarism at the Academy.

The cyberwart finished off the triple hot swiffer. 'I'm sorry to be so direct. Before I say anything else, you must understand that what I am going to tell you is to your advantage. Oh, and allow me to introduce myself. Jason Amrake."

They shook hands, and then Amrake gently led Harris over to a quiet booth, ordering a round of drinks along the way. He spoke in soft, hushed tones, endeavoring to calm the cyberengineer's frazzled nerves. Harris remained passive, not sure whether at any moment he would collapse from a neuronomy or holler for the police. For the time being, he listened. He had the same attachment to Amrake as one might have to a swindling innkeeper in a strange town—he's still the only friend you have.

"Harris, have you ever been to CityTech?"

"No," replied the WestTecher, never having had the opportunity to visit the planet's most prestigious zone.

"I can assure you of one thing: the Triple M will belong to CityTech."

Harris fastened his stare upon the edge of the table.

Amrake ploughed forward. "So I suppose Beecely didn't tell you about the power problems over here."

Harris's face froze at the mention of the name.

"It figures. I used to work with the guy, when I was an intern at CloneFarm. Then he went after the whole bunga at InterFun, and I went to the City. Now I'm with an outfit called BrainHost." Amrake paused to collect his thoughts. "Yeah, I spent most of my career in WestTech. We probably know a lot of the same people."

Harris decompressed a notch, by his own reckoning just out of neuronomy range. He was fascinated by Amrake and the world he represented. Drawing upon his own inside information about cyberbiological projects at CityTech in general and BrainHost in particular, Harris tested the veracity of his interlocutor's story. It all checked out. There was no question in Harris's mind that Amrake moved in the highest technological circles of CityTech.

Amrake did not relent. "BrainHost has a compound, a testing facility, about fifty miles from here. It's part of a TransTech enclave, and heavily guarded. Let me bring you out there for the evening. And," he added with a grin, "just remember—if anything happens to you, the synchbox is useless. So I gotta treat you well."

Harris took a sip of his cephanil freeze, let out a sigh, and glanced at the lighting fixtures above the bar. Was it true that Beecely knew about the power failures? If so, why wasn't he told? Harris juxtaposed the gravity of the mission with the flimsiness of the security arrangements. And perhaps his monetary compensation wasn't all that great either. As for Amrake, what was his plan? If he simply wanted to buy the synchbox, he could do it right there. Harris could feel himself hunched over in his seat, as if pressed down from the weight of the questions.

Amrake expounded on the mediocrity of WestTech, the glory of CityTech, and the never-ending machinations of Beecely. He alleged that at CloneFarm, the noted cyberscientist had had three young and promising research assistants fired and disgraced in order to cover up for his own ineptitude in the Singing Frog scandal, as it came to be known in WestTech.

Harris, of course, was well aware of the incident, and listened intently to Amrake's every word on the subject. "Yeah, at InterFun we suffer from the same kind of back-biting and endless intrigue."

"I know what you're going through over there," said Amrake, "because you're me, five years ago." Harris looked at the skin on Amrake's head and neck. Its perfection was astonishing even to the WestTecher, who had seen the results of countless surgical and chemical procedures for skin flattening. There was something in the utter perfection of Amrake's appearance that was simultaneously irksome and seductive. Harris was succumbing to his fascination with the forbidden fruit.

The helicopter ride to the BrainHost compound was brief and almost without conversation. Harris sat alone in the rear seat, behind the pilot and a cool and collected Amrake. As he gazed out the window, a distinct sentiment emerged. It was a combination of a harsh disdain for his origins and a sense of adventure concerning his destination. He had never taken such a bold step, so completely out of the blue. Over the course of his life, Harris had always been a passive observer, a bystander. Events occurred, and he absorbed the impact. He was unfamiliar with the taste of audacity.

Amrake and the pilot exchanged a few words as they gestured toward a point on the ground a few degrees to starboard. Harris saw the compound approaching. It was smaller and flatter than he had expected. It resembled a fort, square in shape, with a large central courtyard. Outside the exterior wall was a buffer zone enclosed by thick barbed wire and interspersed with sentry towers. Harris surmised that most of the facility was underground.

The helicopter descended onto a pad within the interior yard. After landing, Amrake and his guest moved quickly into the complex. Harris was surprised at the sparse decor in the corridors. The walls and doors, though solid, were simple and unadorned. Amrake opened one of the doors, and they stepped into a conference room. Again, the room was simple, containing a long elliptical table surrounded by about two dozen armchairs. Harris noted the state-of-the-art communications equipment at each post, as well as the elaborate hexaflash rig at the front of the room. His survey was interrupted by the opening of the door behind them.

"Harris," said Amrake with a restrained grin, "I'd like you to meet the CEO of BrainHost, Megan Bullock."

The astonishment on Harris's face could be seen a mile away. Bullock had acquired mythic proportions across the TransTech world. It was no less than meeting the champion, a demigod, an icon to cyberwarts everywhere. She looked different than how Harris had pictured her—stronger, trimmer, and smoother. Her finely-tailored snapsuit accentuated her small but muscular limbs. Her breasts seemed as two round lumps of muscle, her belly an iron plate. A short crop of hair looked as though it has been glued to her scalp, every millimeter perfectly manicured and symmetrical.

Bullock soaked up Harris's worshipful look. "So here you are. Very good. Would you join us for dinner?" Without waiting for a reply, she ushered the two underlings into an adjoining room. Harris noticed the CEO's unusual gait—a steady, swayless motion, like a narrow refrigerator being wheeled across the floor. Her every gesture exuded super-confidence and virility.

They took their appointed seats. The table was set, the food ready. The leader called for the festive meal to commence. Several minutes were spent discussing mundane affairs, such as impressions of Jeptathia and the history of the compound. The three worked their way through the meal, which Harris noted was exclusively biogenerative. At the dessert—a pink sandlubber with a multiplankton crust—Bullock broached the topic at hand.

"Harris, you know as well as I do that we could have just made you a nice, fat offer for the synchbox. Now of course we want it. But we also want *you*." She calmly resumed the consumption of her sandlubber, as if nothing of importance had been said.

Amrake took up the slack. "Harris, isn't it true that you worked on the heliovision project in your early days at InterFun?"

"Well, yes," replied Harris, feeling embarrassed. "But the project was scrapped."

"Hmm," acknowledged Amrake, assuming the grave tone of voice he had used at the hotel bar. "Isn't it true that you are one of the world's leading experts on the underlying technology?"

"Sure, but it's sort of like being a leading expert in internal combustion engines."

Bullock stepped in for the coup de grâce. "Harris, in CityTech we're working on heliovision just as hard as on the Triple M. It's true that the Triple M will establish the supremacy of BrainHost. But heliovision will make it permanent. Have I made myself clear?"

Amrake described, in general terms, their plans to secure domination of the market and marginalize the other sectors of the TransTech world.

"I'm afraid I can't provide any further details right now," he added. "But you'll know everything soon enough."

The scientific side of things did have a certain logic, thought Harris, although the overall plan seemed far-flung. In any case, he need not concern himself with all that. If they wanted to make heliovision a priority, with him as an integral component, who was he to prophesize? Harris could feel his ego inflating. It was true, there were really only two or three others in the world who could match his expertise in heliovision.

He considered the prospect of going to CityTech. Never having been there, his impressions of the mecca of the TransTech world were formed entirely from films, news clips, photos, and anecdotes. Since its inception some eight years previously, CityTech served as a beacon and a model to cyberwarts everywhere. Harris recalled the excitement and hope that infused the globe when CityTech was inaugurated. The urban agglomeration was constructed, from the very first brick, entirely in accordance with the principles of the TransTech Charter. He had always dreamed of going there, but could not easily afford such an expensive trip. He hoped, in vain, that his company would send him to CityTech for a conference or some other assignment.

The three associates capped off the meal with some excellent cognac. After a round of anecdotes about the provincial life of WestTech, Bullock took leave of the two cyberwarts. "I have another meeting," she announced, her facial expression remaining constant. "I'll leave you two to work out the details." She left the room.

A short while later, Amrake escorted Harris to the leisure center. They took a seat at the bar. A number of other BrainHost employees were chatting in small groups, enjoying a relaxing evening. Over hot swiffers, Amrake unveiled his grand design for Harris's immediate transfer to CityTech. No detail had been neglected: He would arrive to find a luxurious, fully-equipped apartment in the prestigious Browser Beach neighborhood; two weeks (on the payroll) to get settled and organized; a private hypercush (uncommon even in CityTech); a visit to Amrake's tailor for a complete new wardrobe in the latest CityTech haute couture; a salary triple his current one; and numerous other perks. A relocation company would pick up his belongings and ship them to his new home.

Amrake's super-smooth face had a look of urgent expectation. Harris took a deep breath and settled far back into the chair, folding his arms and focusing his sight on his knees. Events were happening too fast for him. On the other hand, he reckoned, what luck! This is the kind of opportunity that occurs—if at all—once in a lifetime. But what about the synchbox? Could InterFun take legal action? Technically speaking, yes, but they would never do it, for fear of publicity. Doing business with outerwarts for the delivery of lumber was one thing, but for a piece of cybertechnology? Having their CEO jailed for murder, thought Harris, would be less embarrassing for a major WestTech technology company. It was, however, conceivable that InterFun might quietly seek revenge for his absconding with the synchbox. But it seemed that he couldn't be touched in CityTech—the very bosom of cyberpower. Anyway, it was fairly certain that InterFun would be given a respectable chunk of the Triple M action, albeit in a supporting role. And when heliovision hit the streets, everyone will have forgotten the Triple M.

He sat up straight, looked Amrake in the eye, and vigorously nodded his consent. The two cohorts raised their drinks to toast the new order. "Harris, you are moving into a new echelon," proclaimed Amrake. "And it's going to make us both very happy."

Barely an hour later, the duo embarked on their trip to CityTech. The helicopter whisked them to a nearby airfield, where a corporate jet awaited them. Harris was in awe. He had flown in an airplane only once, as a child. That of course was before the Division, when regular civilian flights were more common. The interior of the jet was the last word in elegance. The space could comfortably accommodate up to twenty or even twenty-five people, in a variety of spaces: work cubicles, small conferencing areas, and dining tables. Amrake led the awe-struck WestTecher to one of the conferencing areas, where they were served light refreshments by the steward.

After receiving an urgent call from the CFO regarding a BrainHost financial matter, Amrake excused himself and headed for one of the work cubicles. Harris gazed out the window at the starry sky, reflecting on the tumultuous events that had turned his life upside down. He certainly had no regrets about leaving InterFun, or even WestTech for that matter. He had no good friends or romantic entanglements to speak of, having lived a fairly solitary existence since graduating from the Academy eight years previously. Most of his relatives were deceased, and he had lost touch with the rest. Harris was an only child. Before the Division, his father was a geologist at an environmental consulting firm, and his mother worked part-time as a customer service representative. Both the consulting firm and their home were destroyed in the Bombardments, and his father never found employment of a quality even remotely resembling his previous post. After several years of declining health and increasing poverty, they rented a room in a boarding house. Several years later, both parents died of natural causes within a short time of each other.

Looking down at the tiny lights on the ground, his thoughts turned to his new position. Yes indeed, he was arriving in grand style. Just think of it—leading the heliovision research effort. Press conferences, consultations with the scientific elite, outrageously savage vacations wherever his heart desired, not to mention outings at the best clubs in CityTech. Harris involuntarily raised his hand to cover his mouth, which was taking the form of an ever-broadening smirk. To see the look on Mandrake's face when she hears the news! No more of those horrendous torture sessions in the chair next to the crustacean. No more lectures about how good his work is, but we're closing that project, etc., etc.

Harris let his head sink into the back of the chair. He soon fell into a profound slumber.

CHAPTER THREE

▼

He awoke to the rising sun reflecting off the wing of the jet, which was taxiing toward a hangar at the main CityTech air facility. Harris strained to shake off his nocturnal haze, to focus on Amrake's eager grin. The latter motioned with outstretched palm toward the window in a silent but hearty announcement of the arrival. Harris mustered a barely perceptible smile as he straightened himself in the seat.

The WestTecher was still in a daze as his companion hurried him from the jet into a standporter, which brought them to an awaiting hypercush. A coterie of personnel buzzed around them, conferring with each other, with Amrake, and with persons unseen. Harris slid inside the vehicle, as if carried along by a force not his own.

The land journey began. The CityTech veteran, smile pasted firm, instructed the debutant. "I know you're a bit overwhelmed by the whole trip. But the beauty of it is, you don't have to push yourself. Take it easy for a few days. Enjoy the town."

Harris was only half concentrating, eager as he was, despite his fatigue, to grab his first views of CityTech. He was fascinated by the multiple stimuli of the vast transport hub, which made the air facilities of WestTech look like a dirt landing strip in the middle of the woods.

"Oh, and one little detail. I think it would be best if I hold onto the synchbox. Just to be on the safe side. Then I'll swing by your place tomorrow to activate it." Harris transferred possession of the valuable jewel, agreeing with the idea but still feeling reticent.

The CityTech landscape presented itself to Harris's avid eyes. He was astonished by the visibility, the air being crystal clear. He recognized elements of the much-heralded Dynamic Node plan by which CityTech was laid out: pentagonal activity nodes, precisely six miles across, separated by interim spaces for a distance of twelve miles. The activity nodes contained several ten-story office buildings, each surrounded by lower satellite structures. All of the construction had generous helpings of glass and steel. The two materials blended together seamlessly, producing a stunning visual effect. The interim spaces consisted of vast manicured gardens interspersed with luxurious, elongated houses. The transition from node to interim space was abrupt and complete, with no intermediate mode of construction. In this regard, it was reminiscent of the walled cities of the ancient world, with their unmistakable division between urban and rural. The entire spectacle was much more impressive than Harris had imagined. In his eyes it was, quite simply, paradise.

He saw on the navizoom that the hypercush was crossing into the activity node known as Browser Beach. He wondered where the beach was, being that CityTech was far inland, the only bodies of water being artificial ponds in the interim spaces. After a couple of turns, they ramped up onto a hypercush port on the mezzanine level of Blue Complex, a residential-commercial cluster.

"Here we are," confirmed Amrake. "Your new home is B-23. The neurolock is set to your personal profile. The computer should be ready. The bar is fully stocked. There's plenty of new clothes. Your consumption account is packed. Relax, take a walk around the complex, be a king."

Harris nodded, opened the jumphatch, and stepped out of the vehicle.

"I almost forgot," said Amrake, poking his head out. "Your personal hypercush is in this port, on ramp seventeen. Have fun." Harris watched his benefactor vanish. He wondered where Amrake had obtained the classified personal data needed for the neurolock. Leave it to the folks at CityTech, he laughed to himself.

The new citywart stepped into the standporter. The machine transported him horizontally and vertically through the building, and deposited him at his door. It opened automatically upon sensing its new master. Harris stepped inside, and was dumbstruck. Nothing he had ever seen in WestTech matched the splendor of his new abode. There was no clash in either color, shape, or dimension. Everything was colored in tones of gray. As far as devices and conveniences were concerned, Harris concluded that nothing was lacking.

He showered, dressed himself with one of the numerous outfits prestocked in the closet, and then popped some bunga nuts into his mouth. Just enough zap to get reoriented, he figured. He picked up his new wallet from the night table next to the bed, tuned the house controls to maintenance level, and set out to explore Blue Complex.

The construction was immaculate. The interior spaces were bathed in natural light and dotted with gardens, streams, and waterfalls. The atmosphere was serene and soft, with few sharp angles or jutting edges. The luxury was ubiquitous. Boutiques of all varieties beckoned, filled with enticing wares and delicacies of the finest quality.

Feeling hungry, Harris took a seat at a small restaurant called the Sidewalk Café. From his table, he had a perfect view of the concourse. Lunch hour was beginning, and soon people were flowing across. They looked polished and streamlined. The women were taut and thin, and they walked with a brisk gait. Harris remarked to himself that by comparison, Bettina Mandrake resembled a wretched outerwart who never had a single skin flattening.

He was struck by the friendliness of the people he encountered during his afternoon promenade. The waiter at the café, for example, could not do enough to please his new customer. People smiled at every opportunity. The only thing that irked Harris slightly was that their eyes never seemed to be completely focused. This made communication a bit more cumbersome than usual. But it was a mere detail compared with his overall positive impression.

After returning to his apartment, Harris checked the computer. A message from Amrake indicated that he would be arriving within the hour to sort out a few formalities. In the meantime, Harris treated himself to a mild mood hookup.

His new CityTech mentor arrived as sleek and well-oiled as ever. They made their way to the telelink room, a state-of-the-art remote workstation that Harris had yet to explore. "Let's take care of the synchbox, just to get it out of the way," said Amrake. He pulled the box out of his pocket and set it on the table. "Just for good business procedure—did you get a chance to look around, find your wallet, consult the computer, see your accounts?"

Harris nodded.

"And you noticed that all contracts and ownership are in order?"

"Oh, absolutely." It was all true, he reckoned; everything he was promised had been executed to the letter.

They concluded the activation of the synchbox, and several other assorted business matters. "This calls for a celebration," declared Amrake. "But not here. Would you do me the honor of joining me at the Hyperclub?"

Harris's mouth nearly dropped. He was being invited to one of the most famous gathering places in the TransTech world, the stuff of legends.

"I guess that means yes. I'll see you there, say, at ten-thirty this evening?"

"Uh...yes...yes, of course."

"And by the way," added Amrake as he was almost out the door, "stop by my tailor. I sent his coordinates to your navizoom. He's expecting you. Hector Smith's the name. Give him a good tip."

That evening, Harris, with great anticipation, climbed aboard his hypercush. What luck, he thought, that Amrake had made all these arrangements. Otherwise, he would feel extremely uncomfortable at the Hyperclub. Even with the proper clothing, he would probably seem out of place, given his provincial speech patterns, skin quality, and mannerisms.

At the tailor's boutique, he slipped into a tapered hammersuit, a rather pricey garment that had been preselected and paid for. All that remained were some slight adjustments. As Harris rotated the view of himself in the autoscope, he was amazed at how thin and elongated he looked. It was exactly his size yet uncomfortable, especially when he slouched. Smith the tailor went about his business efficiently and quietly, never looking directly at the cyberwart. He himself was wearing a bright orange snapsuit that was so tight, Harris wondered how he could open or close it.

Arrangements were made to deliver three or four other suits. Harris tipped him as instructed, to which the suitmaker responded with a small pout, as if to say, "don't think I'm not aware that you're new around here."

On his way to the Hyperclub, Harris's eyes eagerly received the visual datastream. The club was located in Mount Pixel, a different activity node, so it was necessary to cross the twelve miles of interim space. The closer he came, the more elegant the landscaping, and the greater the distance between the houses. He could see no other land use than residential, leading him to surmise that all other activities take place in the nodes. Over the stretch of land that he traversed, he saw only two or three people.

The hammersuit was starting to annoy him, particularly the section around the bottom of his left shoulder blade. Several times he reached around in a futile effort to mollify the fabric by twisting and kneading it. Each time, it rebounded to its former state. The suit exuded an unpleasant chemical odor.

The navizoom showed twenty-eight seconds to Mount Pixel. Harris wondered where the "mount" was, the instruments showing barely an anthill across the entire area. As he entered the activity node, the transition between vegetation and concrete was, as always, abrupt. Mount Pixel looked like Browser Beach, only better. The chosen decor had a reddish-brown color scheme, with abundant brickwork. Every single object—the street fixtures, the standporters, hypercushes, boutiques, gardens, ornamental dogs—was among the most impeccable of its kind. There was not so much as a hair out of place; no litter, no dirt, no grime.

He deposited the hypercush at the Hyperclub's port, exiting the vehicle precisely on schedule. He had timed his arrival at the front door of the club for one minute fifteen seconds prior to the rendezvous. A crowd about a dozen thick was milling about, just outside the main entrance. Harris stationed himself at an observation point at the edge of the human mass. Now he could see why the hammersuit was so crucial. It seemed outrageous to him, but compared to what the others were wearing, his was among the more subdued and comfortable-looking outfits. Some of the garb was unlike anything he had ever seen in WestTech. One woman was dressed with narrow strips of treaded rubber, clasped to her body by means of a transparent plastic cord wound around the shoulders.

At the appointed meeting time, Amrake was just breaching the far edge of the crowd. Harris noticed a woman at his side. From the outset, there was no question that she was his absolute preferred female type: short, with olive-colored skin, pronounced lips, and long black hair. She was full-bodied but not overweight.

"Harris," said Amrake, "I hope you don't mind that I brought a friend."

The WestTecher's pleasant facial expression provided an unambiguous sign of consent.

"Say hello to Angela Templeton. Angela, this is Harris."

"Nice to meet you."

"Nice to meet you."

After a few moments of small talk, Amrake ushered them into the club. In the crowded entranceway, Harris popped some bunga nuts into his mouth. His gaze shifted back and forth from the surrounding environment to the various parts of Templeton's body. Did she belong to Amrake? What did Amrake mean by "a friend"? Harris had rather detached himself from male-female bonding for several years, but this was beyond his power of detachment. It was as if his deepest, most primordial lusts had been served up in a custom-made specimen.

The three of them sat down at one of the many small tables. Templeton excused herself for a moment. Amrake gestured in her direction with his eyebrows. "So, what do you think? Is she your type, or what?" There was a mischief that radiated from his eyes across his entire face, as if to say, there's something sinfully delicious about to take place here, and it's all premeditated. "I had a feeling she'd be right. She's yours, my friend. Strike up a little conversation, and then pack her into your cush. I have to get back to the office for a late meeting with the boss."

While they waited, Harris absorbed the atmosphere of the legend that was the Hyperclub. He recalled the day that Mandrake had returned from a trip to CityTech. She extolled the club's famous Sensitivity Window. Sitting within spitting distance of the monument, Harris for once found himself in agreement with his former boss. He was duly impressed: The massive vitrine, some thirty yards long and ten deep, portrayed scenes from an epic poem by one of CityTech's leading literary figures, Hans Slydebergen. The scenes were performed live in six simultaneous vignettes that were repeated every fifteen minutes. The story involved the transcendental plateau reached by the hero, an adolescent boy, as he discovers the multiple facets of his sexual awakening. The highlight of the spectacle, by popular consensus, was the scene where the boy becomes a shepherd, and then falls in love with one of his lambs.

The vitrine was bathed in a flickering pink neon light. The frequency of the flickering coincided with the beat of the jolt music available at each seat. The on-off switch was located on the side of the armrest. When activated, the low bass pounding was heard at an extremely high volume, but only within a one-foot radius of the seat. Thus a person passing through one of the club's dark walkways did so in silence, apart from the background din of conversation. The seat itself contracted and expanded to the beat, and with each contraction sent a mild electric shock into the body of its occupant. Harris activated the jolt. Amrake smiled as he watched his protégé grip the armrests as if he were riding in an airplane that had fallen into a nose-dive.

Amrake motioned with his thumb at the approaching Templeton, and Harris switched off the jolt. "Don't worry, old boy," said Amrake, "you can come back here whenever you want. I set up a twenty percent discount for you—special deal for BrainHost executives."

The goddess returned. Every inch of Harris's body was awash in desire. He could not recall the last time he had been overcome in such a fashion. The fingernails of his left hand were involuntarily digging into the armrest. A puddle of sweat had formed between the small of his back and the hammersuit.

Amrake got the ball rolling. "Angela also works at BrainHost. She's a dietician. Ask her anything you want about nourishment." He lightly tapped Harris's leg under the table.

Harris awkwardly cleared his throat, and then let it be known, with forced nonchalance, that actually he had been wondering about a few things.

"Really?" said Templeton. "You can ask me, really you can, go ahead." Her monotone speech pattern reminded him of the default voice on his computer at InterFun.

Amrake was looking intense; Harris forced himself to play along. "Is it true," he ventured in a timid voice, "that the furry pig is dangerous to eat?"

"Not at all," declared Templeton. "Just don't eat the glands."

"I see," said Harris, with a prolonged nod.

Amrake's personal datapad began to flash. "Sorry, folks, but duty calls. Go easy on Harris, okay? It's his first night out in CityTech. Oh, and don't worry about the bill. It's on the company." He departed in great haste.

Harris looked at his new playmate. Her skin quality was nearly perfect, just a notch below that of Megan Bullock. There was scant variation in her facial expression, and her eyes were stagnant and cold. He had the impression of being in the company of an elaborate mannequin. The monotone voice announced its master's wishes: "This club has bad air. Jason said you have a hypercush. I'd like to take a ride."

"Sure," said Harris, eager to exit the contrived situation.

In the hypercush, Harris set the navizoom for a random cruise around Mount Pixel, for a duration of seventeen minutes. Again, he pondered the lady wart. Her demeanor left him continually embarrassed and rather bored. But her purely physical aspects highly stimulated his male drives, causing him to feel increasingly suffocated in his hammersuit. He somehow managed some chatter about his favorable impressions of CityTech.

The dietician's responses were flat and brief. At the end of the cruise, she announced her new inclination: "Jason said you live in Blue Complex at Browser Beach. I've never been there."

Twenty minutes later, Harris found himself standing next to the bar in his apartment, with the object of his desire just alongside. He let his right arm extend into her personal space. It was aimed at a small exposed portion of her left shoulder. There was no resistance yet no encouragement. He rested his hand on the skin, which was perfectly flattened.

Templeton channeled the unfolding event onto a verbal track. "That feels good," said the computer sound-alike. "Shall we go to the bedroom and begin the standard procedures?"

Harris was unable to muster a response.

"Jason said you might not be up to speed." She took his hand and led him into the bedroom. "Don't worry. We'll start with an easy one. How far have you gotten in the coital matrix?"

Harris had never heard of such a thing, but was afraid to reveal his ignorance. "I...I don't remember," he stammered. "I think it might have been number twelve."

"That's not bad. We'll have fun. By the way, do you have any thermal spread?" Another item foreign to the WestTecher, who alleged that he didn't get a chance to buy any. Meanwhile, Templeton unzipped her upper garment, exposing her unusually firm breasts. She sat on the bed, and began to conduct calculations on her datapad. Harris, pretending not to notice this behavior, sat down beside her and again released his arm, this time in the direction of the chest. Just short of the target, his arm was knocked aside by a firm blow, causing a bit of a sting and a large dose of embarrassment.

"What are you doing?" she exclaimed, in the evening's first sign of emotion. "We haven't even started the preliminaries." Seeing his condition, she softened somewhat, allowing him to touch her breast, but just briefly. The dietician was gazing at her datapad as the cyberengineer placed his hand on the coveted mammary. It was as cold and hard as the jumphatch of a hypercush. Harris was swept with a morose anxiety, as if he had caressed the tentacles of an octopus. He withdrew his limb.

"Okay," said Templeton, staring into the tiny monitor. "You have to take off your hammersuit, lie across me at a fifteen degree incline, and perform a sideways Sander motion."

Harris forced himself into a semblance of clear thinking, in a last-ditch attempt to salvage the evening. He asked for clarification.

"Here, I'll run a short hexaflash demo. It shows you exactly what to do."

After watching the demo for half a minute, Harris succumbed to another anxiety attack, more severe than the first. This time it was too much. His innards were engulfed in nausea, something akin to food poisoning. Feeling by now quite out of control, he lurched into the bathroom, barely arriving before the spasms of vomiting began. It was not merely physical, but a deep, soulful vomiting, as a dormant nerve was aroused from its slumber.

Harris cleaned himself off and returned to the bedroom. He looked at Templeton. Her brow was slightly contracted, in an offhanded look of concern, as if he had told her that he had a mild headache. He reckoned that she wasn't, after all, a totally heartless creature.

He began dressing himself. "Maybe I got food poisoning, or it's my neuro-intestinitus, which sometimes reacts to cephanil juice," he said.

His partner's silence expressed her disappointment. She solemnly rezipped her suit. Harris tried to pick up the pieces. "I'm really sorry. I just need to recover from my trip, and brush up a bit on my coital matrix."

No sooner had his date departed than Harris parked himself in front of the computer. The cyberengineer set himself to the task of comprehending the sexual rituals of CityTech. He launched a number of queries, and soon pieced together a rough story. The coital matrix, he learned, was invented about five years earlier by a team of researchers at the AntiStress Institute, in Harris's own Browser Beach. It was hailed as the panacea for every variety of sexual malaise. No one would ever have to be confronted with a perplexing or stressful situation: roles, power relations, cues, and guilt would all be eliminated, to be replaced by pure enjoyment and maximum performance, with a minimum of effort. Harris glanced at reviews from CityTech's leading authorities. It was an airtight consensus of approval, with the exception of one or two oblique references to information sources in outerwart territory.

Harris re-evaluated his drastic reaction to the hexaflash demo. Was he just an unsophisticated bumpkin from a remote outpost, going through the motions but actually incapable of internalizing such an advanced lifestyle? Would he fail? Was the entire CityTech adventure an exercise in futility? He remained immobilized for over an hour. Disgusted with himself, he dragged his body to the bed and fell asleep fully dressed.

The next morning, he awoke in a disoriented condition. Instead of awe, his surroundings caused him to feel dread. Everything reminded him of his pitiful state, of his inadequacy. If word got out of his shoddy performance at the bedside, he would most certainly become the laughingstock of any social circle. He marshaled the energy to fight back. No, he resolved, there was no way he would allow this golden opportunity to slip through his fingers. He would study the coital matrix like the engineer he is, and then, if necessary, ingest a large dose of class AA bunga nuts before the act. Presumably, after two or three sessions, he would grow accustomed to the process and eventually enjoy it. This supposition was confirmed by the literature he had perused.

After a mild cerebral plunge, Harris delved into an obsessive frenzy of research, the intensity of which he had not experienced since his days at the Academy. His face glued to the computer, he devoured everything from detailed anatomical analysis to straightforward how-to guides. By the afternoon, he was feeling satisfied with himself, well along the way to snatching victory from the jaws of defeat. Newly defiant, he resolved not only to overcome his fear and revulsion, but to become skilled in the latest methods, mastering the practical as well as the theoretical aspects of the coital matrix.

Harris did not budge from his abode for three days. He communicated occasionally with Amrake, telling him that he was engaged in an impromptu crash course to "learn about the culture and lifestyle of CityTech." On the third day, after consuming a full-course biogenerative lunch delivered from the Sidewalk Café, he contacted Templeton.

"I want to apologize again for that horrible evening," he told his matrix partner. "I think I was very disoriented from my transfer to CityTech. But now I feel much better, having rested for several days. Would you give me another chance, and drop by this evening after you finish work?"

Ten minutes after Templeton's arrival, Harris was in full swing. The bunga had just taken effect. It was a stellar performance. He bravely repelled his fear and revulsion like a medic on the battlefield.

Nothing could be more telling than Templeton's summary of the event: "That was incredible. I never dreamed of doing number ninety-eight before next year. Looks like WestTech isn't as Neanderthal as everyone thinks." She concentrated intently for a moment, then looked up at him. "Listen," she said, "I'm sorry about last time. I shouldn't have been so hard on you. I guess it's because the matrix always goes so smoothly, it's automatic. I never had a problem before. So I got impatient. Sorry."

Harris was only half-listening, glowing as he was with satisfaction over his triumph. "Oh, it's okay," he said. "Don't worry about it."

He looked at her body, and found it still to be in accordance with his taste. Yet his overall attraction had diminished considerably. Indeed, even though his body was drained from the concentrated physical effort, he derived no satisfaction from the act itself. This was to be expected; he recalled from his survey of the literature that the coital matrix had a strong tendency to dampen the male's animalistic, egotistical sexual drive caused by the exclusivist, aggressive desire to possess a unique female and deny affection and caring to other human beings.

He finished dressing, went to the bar, and fixed two swiffer lites. Templeton joined him, and they toasted the "successful debut of their matricing." He took advantage of the good cheer to clarify an issue that was bothering him. "Tell me, Angela," he said. "How did you get to know Jason Amrake?"

The dietician remained calm, but the corners of her mouth betrayed a certain disruption of the nerves. "Oh, I don't know, just from work, here and there." Harris looked at her face. Immediately following the delivery of her deflection, it returned to its usual, doll-like structure. No change in the environment—be it sound, temperature, or human activity—seemed to have any significant affect on her emotional state. Harris envied her self-control, though it tended to limit the extent of most conversations.

"Have you known him a long time?" he said.

"I don't know, a while," she answered. "Do you have any food here?"

"Sure," said Harris. He decided not to push the issue, so as to finish the evening on a positive note. He fed Templeton, and they parted with a firm handshake, as was the CityTech custom.

Harris could hardly contain his joy. He did it! The first major hurdle of the CityTech adventure had been overcome with resounding success. He began pacing to and fro, so infused he was with confidence and enthusiasm. He ventured out into Blue Complex to share his zest for life with the world. As he strolled about, the cyberengineer weighed his options for the rest of the week. There were still several days remaining in his initial adjustment period, and he could use the time to explore other parts of Browser Beach or beyond. But he rejected the idea, instead deciding to begin work as soon as possible. Advancing the schedule would impress people, but more importantly, he would exploit his current super-positive mood. If he waited, his inconsistent neurological tendencies could easily take a turn for the worse. The present feeling might dissipate and be replaced by one of his more anxious moments.

Despite these thoughts, Harris remained at home for one more day, but solely to prepare himself adequately for the crucial first day on the job. He embarked upon a meticulous round of study, reading a wide variety of material on BrainHost, and on the latest developments in heliovision. He carefully selected his garments, choosing the custom-made "boss suit" that Smith the tailor had boasted was one of his finest creations. It was designed to be informal—ostentatiously so—yet it was cut from rare and costly materials that exuded elitism at every stitch. It was a perfect match, Harris reckoned, for BrainHost's highly-touted "hierarchy of informality."

The next morning, Harris's hypercush approached the southwest port of BrainHost's main facility in Deltoid, one of the activity nodes closest to Browser Beach. The former InterFun employee took a deep breath and braced himself for the flurry of activity that was about to take place.

The BrainHost building was one of the most unusual Harris had ever seen, and quite unlike the other structures in CityTech. It had no identifiable shape. Instead, there were wavy, curving "legs" that protruded from a central core. Each leg had a different length, width, and height. Seen from above, the building resembled an amoeba. The arrangement of the floors was quite unorthodox, and it was not possible at first glance to count them. This was because the various layers had flat, horizontal portions as well as diagonal ones, and they intruded into one another. This bizarre effect was amplified by the transparence of the exterior glass wall, exposing everything to the observer.

Waiting at the hypercush port was Harris's new personal assistant, Mr. Helmutsen. This was their first meeting, although they had communicated several times electronically. Helmutsen had been handpicked by Amrake. He had a degree in cybertechnological marketing, and had proven himself adept as a top-notch, getting-the-job-done organizer. As Amrake explained, the personal assistant would handle the administrative details so that Harris could devote his time and energy exclusively to the research effort.

They shook hands and exchanged pleasantries. Harris studied his helper's face. He had the same polished exterior as Amrake, yet his regard was duller, more immobile. Helmutsen was like the sequel to a blockbuster film: The props are still there, but one searches in vain for the spark of genius that made the original movie a success.

They passed through the protective wall that separated the hypercush port from the facility within. It was to be one of several such barriers that Harris would traverse on a daily basis. As they stepped across the security rig, he noticed the elaborate electronic devices, much more rigorous than in WestTech. Apparently, even in CityTech, to which access is strictly controlled, security was taken very seriously.

Harris attracted a number of curious yet icy glances, triggered no doubt by the boss suit. The BrainHost rank-and-file knew nothing of his arrival. In fact, those aware of the event could almost be counted on the fingers of one hand: Amrake, Bullock, Templeton, Helmutsen, and two or three others.

As he strode down the wavy corridor, there seemed to be little sense to the layout, a far cry from the simple rectangle of the InterFun compound back home. The light in the corridor was of an undefinable intensity, giving the eye a sensation that alternated between insufficiency and excess glare, not unlike the nervous glow of an antique computer. Excepting the security rigs, there were no doors to be seen, only portals, as they were called, a square yard or so of floor-to-ceiling hologram that could be configured by the occupant of the adjacent office. Only by virtue of the familiar objects to be seen within the offices was Harris slightly put at ease in the maze.

His eyes were fatigued by the time Helmutsen proudly led him through the portal of the cyberengineer's new home-away-from-home. The hologram was set to simulate the open jaws of a furry pig. After being swallowed whole, as it were, Harris viewed his new office. It was a stark contrast to the common areas of the building. It seemed to him like an extension of Mount Pixel: sublime, harmonious luxury, with a reddish-brown color scheme. A pleasant light emanated from recessed fixtures adjacent to the ceiling. The desk and chair were of a finely-toned mahogany, locking together like a jigsaw puzzle. The sumptuous form of the chair, thought Harris, made the most advanced ergosnap model look like a simple barstool. Off to one side of the room was a recessed mini conference area, with five fully-equipped workstations and simulation helmets. The entire scene was most agreeable to the man in the boss suit.

"Okay, sir," said Helmutsen. "Shall I leave you to get settled in? I'm just next door if you need me." The assistant took leave.

Harris parked his somewhat weary body behind the desk. On the computer, the datapile was crowned by a cheery welcome from the enthusiasm machine himself. Amrake's talking head explained the schedule for the coming week, which included numerous meetings with BrainHost's top management and research personnel. That afternoon featured a session with Megan Bullock and the head of research and development, Alexandra Humboldt-Weizmann. Toward evening, there would be a hexaflash presentation of the company's product line. Amrake would arrive in person one half-hour from the end of Harris's reading of the message.

"You look great," exclaimed Amrake, stepping through the portal two minutes later. "I'm a bit early, but I just had to make sure everything was under control." They shook hands. Harris announced his satisfaction with the new work area.

"It's vital to BrainHost that you have the best conditions," declared Amrake. "Heliovision is critical to our future, and this spot is critical to heliovision." He escorted Harris down the corridor to one of several detensers, or small conferencing points where less formal tasks took place, often with a snack and beverage. The armchairs, as wide and deep as a first-class seat on an airliner, were designed to maintain minimal body tension. They had movable datapads that could be brought to the head in the manner of a spotlight over a dentist's chair.

"I must say," said Harris, "the comfortable, plush offices are so different from the common areas of the building, which are a bit disorienting."

"Yes, we all have to live with that. This topic will come up later in the week when we have discussions with the security people. But I can give you a quick preview."

"Please do."

"All of CityTech has suffered in recent years from periodic breakdowns of security. As you know, after the Division"—Amrake uttered the word in a whisper—"a fierce campaign was waged to clean out the last vestiges of outerwart presence and hermetically seal off the TransTech world. It was even more airtight in CityTech, whose residents came to enjoy the highest level of peace and tranquility. The last two years, however, have seen the advent of *internal* breaches of security. Certain individuals within CityTech, some of them connected to elements across the Line, have tried to smash the CityTech infrastructure and even physically attack our leaders."

Harris felt the day's first surge of unintended muscular contraction. Amrake continued the story. He explained that originally, BrainHost was located at another site in Deltoid, in a tasteful, elegant building that was a landmark of luxury and gracious accommodations. But after progressively more egregious breaches of security, BrainHost abandoned its former facility and constructed its present headquarters. The building was designed with one overriding feature in mind: the safety of its occupants and the integrity of its infrastructure. The winding corridors were meant to frustrate quick movement in and out of the premises, and the strange light was installed to disrupt depth perception and blur any vision beyond one or two yards. In a crisis, it could be set to a variety of effects. The walls contained auraprobes that could locate and then paralyze any living creature. The office interiors, by contrast, were exact replicas of the work space at the old headquarters.

Amrake read the look of distress on Harris's face. "Don't worry, old boy, you just concentrate on your research. We have some fine warts over at security, you'll meet them. There hasn't been a single incident in over six months." This statistic did not prevent Harris from feeling a slight craving for cephanil juice.

That afternoon, Amrake escorted Harris to the chambers of the CEO. The cyberengineer glanced around the room in merry disbelief. He had arrived at a key threshold, the first closed-door session with BrainHost's high command. Seeing Megan Bullock on her own turf, and in a moment of triumph, raised her pedestal to even greater heights. At her side was no less a figure than R&D chief Alexandra Humboldt-Weizmann, inventor of the pitch-and-pull technology that provided a platform for later developments in cyberbiology. In Harris's view, these two warts together accounted for one of the greatest technological revolutions since the semiconductor. Harris felt like a schoolboy who finds himself in the presence of his greatest sports idols. In addition, they were joined by a handful of top engineers, each of whom was endowed with a curriculum vitae that guaranteed its owner a slot in the annals of CityTech.

Bullock was something of an enigma. She was the daughter of two physicians who, during her childhood, circled the globe in search of victims to assist: survivors of floods and famines, refugees, prisoners of war. Bullock had lived in numerous countries and spoke six languages fluently, understanding several others. Her mother, something of a celebrity, served as the first director of international projects in the new CityTech government, while her father managed the worldwide relief organization.

As Harris well knew, Bullock's movement up the CityTech ladder was nothing if not meteoric. Everything she touched turned to success. From the outset, she proved herself an adept administrator as well as a brilliant scientist. The combination was irresistible.

The mystery involved her personal life. She was fairly sociable, showing up regularly at cultural events and gatherings at private homes. But Bullock was never accompanied by an intimate friend. In fact, no one had ever witnessed such an occurrence in all her days at CityTech. It was widely rumored that during this time she had not touched another human being—not even in the framework of the coital matrix.

Bullock kicked off the meeting. She lauded the new catch from WestTech, but omitted any mention of the Triple M equations, or indeed of the entire Jeptathia affair. Harris was presented simply as a great engineer and innovator who decided to make a career switch. She noted his expertise in heliovision, and then mocked InterFun's decision to drop their own heliovision research. The CEO then turned the floor over to Humboldt-Weizmann.

Harris was distracted by her appearance. Humboldt-Weizmann was in her mid forties, thin and strong, but not muscular. Her hair was short and closely cropped, but not ironed down like Bullock's. There were no traces of cosmetics. The facial features were angular and jagged, with a bark-like texture. Her thin mouth resembled a crack in the side of a tree. Her upper body, flat as an ironing board, jerked suddenly from side to side, before the arrival of the face at the final point of motion. The voice was gruff, with just a trace of the feminine. Harris could not recall seeing a less attractive woman.

These observations did not interfere, however, with the glow of Humboldt-Weizmann's speech, which was eloquent and eminently informed. She possessed the quiet self-confidence of the true expert. Harris was in awe: Just think, this would be his primary collaborator. What a difference from Mandrake, who was a functionary par excellence, rising through the ranks by uttering platitudes such as "the inevitable triumph of the Triple M." But here was a colleague worthy of the name.

Humboldt-Weizmann addressed the key issues involved in the heliovision effort, including the top security involved. Only those present would be privy to the full story whereas others would be informed on an as-needed basis, receiving their personal assignment without necessarily being apprised that it involved heliovision. She expected that the alpha version would be ready four months hence, with a full production version of the product "out the door" no later than seven months down the line. This was a dense schedule, and critical to the ascendancy of BrainHost. Certain key field operations were already in progress, and their success was contingent upon the integrity of the deadlines. Amrake added that the compensation package accompanying a punctual and successful completion of the project would be "sweeter than sweet."

Over the next few days, Harris became acquainted with all that was BrainHost. On more than one evening, a double cerebral plunge was necessary to unwind, such were the pressure and long hours to which he was subjected. Nevertheless, it pleased him greatly. He was well received, respected, and for the first time in his career, using his full mental capacity. In short, Harris had been catapulted from obscurity in a TransTech backwater to a highly-visible position near the top of the CityTech pyramid.

By the end of the week, however, Harris was laden with stress. He felt the tension throughout his neck and back as he left the office. In need of diversion, he took a stroll through Blue Complex. The streams and waterfalls helped to ameliorate the problem. He came upon a posh art gallery, which presented the opportunity to forget his workaday troubles and at the same time become better acquainted with a facet of elite CityTech culture.

His toe was barely across the threshold when he was greeted by a young woman, thin and bald, with enormous breasts lifted and framed by a gold-plated plasticase. The exposed nipples glowed from a phosphorescent coating. Harris found it difficult to look directly at her, if only because he could not gauge the appropriate distance at which to stand.

Seeing his boss suit, she outdid herself with effusive greetings and offers of assistance before turning Harris loose to "browse at your own leisure." In the first of several large rooms, he could not ascertain whether a rusty ergosnap chair, occupying one side of the room all by itself, was an exhibit. But moving closer, he perceived a small label next to it on the wall:

LE SNAP DE LA VIE, Antoinette Babcock, collage in metal and leather. Rare. Produced just before the artist's death, it is considered to be one of the finest examples of the protosemiunrealism school.

Harris understood nothing of this. Seeing from the corner of his eye that he was under observation, he stepped back from the object, stroked his chin, and let out a prolonged "hmmm."

The next room, larger than the first, was totally bare. He looked to one side and then the other, thinking he was missing something. He began moving closer to the far side, when the young lady suddenly shouted, "Stop! Don't move!" She ran up to him, as if to bar his path with her own body. "Sorry to startle you, sir, but you were about to step on a Labambini."

Harris looked down to see, inches from his foot, a small piece of paper upon which was written THIS ROOM IS EMPTY. Alongside the words was an illegible signature.

"It's not often one runs across a signed Labambini, heh heh" said the young woman with a smile, trying to lighten up the situation and put her potential client at ease. Harris inquired as to the price of the work. The figure given was six times his annual salary. "The price includes the services of an artistic adviser, who comes to your house to help you find just the right spot for it."

He thanked the young lady and exited the gallery.

This experience whet Harris's appetite for cultural outings. The opportunity was not long in coming. He was beside himself with satisfaction when Bullock invited him to accompany her and Humboldt-Weizmann to one of the major cultural events of the season: a gala concert performed by the CityTech Symphony Orchestra. Harris had never attended a classical concert, and was quite curious to experience it.

The BrainHost trio needed fifteen minutes to make their way from the front door of the concert hall to their seats in the first row of the dress circle. In the lobby and along the stairs, the CEO and R&D chief pressed the flesh, introducing Harris to a variety of business and personal acquaintances. When finally they stepped into the auditorium, he was quite impressed. The colossal theater, seating about ten thousand, was decorated in shades of CityTech gray, something akin to Harris's apartment. Hanging from the ceiling was an electric guitar, some fifty feet in length, suspended on invisible cables so that it seemed to hover above the audience's heads. On the ceiling itself was a huge pentaflash screen displaying the greatest musicians of all time, a different one every half second.

When they arrived at their places, the spectacle was about to begin. Harris looked at the program that had been loaded automatically into his datapad:

SCHUBERT'S EIGHTH SYMPHONY: FINALLY FINISHED !

A contemporary interpretation, conducted by Heather Fuller-Morris

Hypertone solo: Ransanavalana Tevel

Harris wondered what a hypertone was. He was soon to find out. The lights dimmed. Suddenly, as if by magic, the orchestra appeared on the stage. "Nice stealthing effect," he whispered to Humboldt-Weizmann, impressed with the stunt that was much crisper and sharper than when he had seen it done in WestTech. The CityTech Symphony was a standard classical orchestra, dressed in the traditional black and white garb. The musicians tuned their instruments. The conductor entered the scene, to tumultuous applause. She looked to be in her mid twenties.

Her minimalist couture featured a diamond-studded plasticase (more elaborate than the one in the art gallery, noted Harris) containing a tiny hexaflash device that emitted musical notes from the area of the nipples.

The applause faded into a hush. On the left side of the stage, a segment of the floor slid open, and up rose a platform containing Ransanavalana Tevel and his hypertone. The instrument was a gray box with a lever on top, resembling a throttle. The musician was naked and hairless, his entire body painted the same gray color as the box. The applause was even louder and of longer duration than before. When it subsided, Fuller-Morris tapped the podium with her tiny baton, and motioned delicately to her right. The bass section played the opening notes of Schubert's eighth symphony, which was followed by total silence. The conductor, with a grave visage, oscillated her left arm tempestuously in the direction of Tevel. The latter slowly pushed the throttle forward. The audience was seized with rapt anticipation. Little by little, a throbbing bassline increased in intensity until the entire house literally shook from the intermittent thump. Harris's entrails jumped at each beat. Some members of the audience began vomiting. Fortunately, special receptacles had been installed in the back of the seats for just this contingency.

The orchestra then played the remaining twenty-two and a half minutes of the symphony. The music was barely audible behind the incessant pounding of the hypertone. In the final minute, the blasts increased in frequency, ending in ten seconds of machine-gun rapidity.

During the long round of applause, Bullock glanced at Harris with a look of smug satisfaction, conveying the unmistakable message, "you're at the top, my friend."

Chapter Four

▼

In addition to a solid cultural education, not to be neglected was Harris's assimilation into the appropriate social circles, for the sake of his own happiness as well as for the cohesion of the BrainHost elite. Soon after the concert, he was invited to a Sunday picnic at the home of William Nice III, the billionaire construction magnate, chairman of the board of BrainHost and builder of the headquarters complex. His home, a myriad of structures resting on a two hundred acre estate, was located in the Electric Lake interim space, just alongside the Deltoid activity node. The gathering was known to be one of the prime social events of the year.

"Harris, you're going to love it," said a beaming Amrake in Harris's office on the Friday before the picnic. "Everyone'll be there: the boss, Humboldt-Weizmann, money people, political people, you name it. You can network till you drop." He then described the expected entertainment, taking place at multiple points in the Nice compound, and the bar, whose description made Harris's eyes open to maximum aperture. He was convinced that the party's host would leave no stone unturned in his preparations, and that the brain fulfillment would be unrivaled.

Despite the anticipated level of enjoyment, Harris felt a twinge of apprehension at being thrown in with the lions, as it were. Once again, he feared high society's reaction to his simple, provincial origins. There was still so much about CityTech that he did not know or did not understand. The risk of committing a faux pas loomed large.

On Sunday, Amrake escorted Harris to the Nice estate. They parked the hypercush in the underground port just inside the main gate, resurfaced, and then strolled across the hundred yards or so of gardens and fountains that led up to the mansion. Amrake led the cyberengineer through the foyer and into the main hall. The interior lighting alternated between a kaleidoscope effect, with colors of varying brightness shooting in rays across the space, and blinding flashes of white light. As for the architecture and decor, it was the epitome of eclecticism. There were masses of decorative objects, each hand-picked from among the finest specimens on the market. These included statues from Crete, mosaics from Pompeii, Ming vases, Aztec fertility goddesses, voluminous Empire-style silver wine coolers by Odiot, sumptuous art nouveau armchairs by Van de Velde, blue-period Picassos, and pulsating emeraldine lamps by CityTech's own Labambini.

Harris's initial glimpse of the event left him with his mouth agape. The sensation was that of arrival, as if his entire life were nothing more than a corridor leading into the grand concourse that was this sublime celebration. The parties at the Coast, the amphidrome at Clickville, every potion he ever imbibed at a bar were all mere sparks alongside the great inferno.

A rude but light slap on the back snapped him out of his reverie. "Harris, are you there?" grinned Amrake. "I keep telling myself that you're gonna love it in CityTech. I can see it in your eyes—you're one of us."

The two warts stepped up to the bar, which offered the most deluxe brain-fulfillment substances available on the planet. Harris was like a kid in a candy store as Amrake reviewed the menu. They spent a good half hour sampling the various delights before proceeding deeper into the festivities.

At the flanks of the hall were steps descending into subterranean amphidromes. Harris and Amrake spent several minutes in each one. The first drome contained dive-bombing, viewed by audiences shrieking in ecstasy. The next one featured flying platforms with human and beast engaged in every manner of union, with audience members scooped up from their seats to participate in the act. Yet another drome contained a rapid-fire hexaflash spectacle showing the latest experiments in coital methodology, with live demonstrations blending in and becoming indistinguishable from the hexaflash version. The amphidromes, however, were only the hors d'oeuvre. The main dish was yet to come.

Harris experienced a tingling sensation in his extremities. His blood pressure was dropping. His head felt as if it were separated from his body and encased in gel, sealed off from contact with the world. Like a fish out of water, his lungs gasped for air, yet his body was so numb that he felt no discomfort. How strange, thought Harris, that he was experiencing what was said to be the initial effect of the Triple M.

And if heliovision made Triple M look like child's play, as Humboldt-Weizmann put it, he wondered what a human body and mind would look like after receiving the full dose. Harris fully agreed with the claims made by Bullock that heliovision would produce a superior being, a mind that could "see" farther than any previously, exceeding the wildest dreams of any guru, shaman, or philosopher. It was a daunting prospect, seductive yet terrifying in its perfection.

The two cohorts emerged into the daylight of the giant yard behind the main hall. Harris turned his deeply introspective countenance toward his guide.

"Hey, pull yourself together," said Amrake. "Save some energy for later. You look like you've been run over by a steamroller. Anyway, we need to decide where to go." He had an unusually concerned look. "Harris, are you ready to go all the way yet? I mean, to see the absolute peak of CityTech life? It's taking place about two hundred yards from here. Humboldt-Weizmann and the boss should be arriving there shortly, and Nice himself is running the show."

Harris knew what he had to do. This was another test of his mettle, similar to his comeback on the coital matrix with Templeton. If he was to join this elite, and take full advantage of the magnificent opportunity, then he had to fuse himself to them, to embrace their lifestyle and world view. Merely showing up for work every morning would be insufficient.

He nodded his consent to Amrake.

The two elite warts stepped into a standporter, which transported them across the broad central yard. The verdant expanse contained varying styles of gardens set back from a central promenade. Some of the gardens were modeled after the finest European exemplars, while others featured small zoos.

The standporter came to a stop in front of the crown jewel of the Nice estate: the Dome of Ascent. Its form resembled a mushroom, with a narrow, white marble base supporting a glass-covered dome some eighty yards in diameter. The external sheet of glass had the tint and consistency of the finest pinkish-white pearl, and exuded a soft glow that made it impossible for the eye to identify its precise boundary.

Another standporter soon arrived, carrying the CEO and the head of R&D. Harris viewed their entrance onto the scene: Both women were wearing elegant, flowing red silk robes. Others guests, dressed in an identical manner, filed into the bottom of the mushroom. There was an awkward silence as the four elite cyberwarts stood face-to-face in front of the sanctuary.

Bullock broke the ice, addressing herself to Amrake. "Jason, did you bring your blood robe?"

"No," he replied, putting his arm around Harris. "Today I'm keeping an eye on this guy. He's too valuable to be left alone. I thought we would go up to the balcony for a few minutes, just to take a look."

Bullock's icy visage thawed one degree as she looked Harris up and down. "That would be fine, and you are welcome to stay as long as you want, robe or no robe." The BrainHost CEO resumed her usual refrigerator-like movement, rolling into the mushroom with Humboldt-Weizmann in tow. The two subordinates followed, and then took an elevator up to the balcony. From there, they had a commanding view of the amphitheater.

There were thirty plush, red armchairs in five graduated semicircular rows, all facing west. Each was separated from its neighbors by a curtain of light. In front of the armchairs was a control panel, with a datapad, a mood hookup, and other devices. The ceiling was imbued with the same pearly translucent glow as was the exterior of the building. Just below the fringe of the ceiling was a frieze about five feet wide that portrayed the history of spiritual and occult powers, featuring such luminaries as Terah, Balaam, Nostradamus, and Houdini. The center and lowest point of the amphitheater contained a cylindrical platform, about eight feet in diameter and four feet high, in solid steel with a matte titanium finish. Next to the platform, on its eastern side, was an armchair slightly larger than the others. It was here that the chairman presided.

The spectacle that ensued amplified Harris's sensation of a gelled and disconnected head. There was a blinding flash of light, after which a human form could be seen lying on the platform. It was not immediately clear whether it was clothed or naked, for its body was smooth and hairless, and seemingly devoid of reproductive organs. It possessed a silky, dull, steel-blue color, with flat, almost imperceptible facial features. There was no way to ascertain its gender.

Harris stood breathless as the human embraced itself. No words have yet been invented to aptly describe the opening and closing of orifices, the manner in which body parts became fully or partially submerged in other parts of its flesh, or the hideous facial contortions that ensued. It was not clear whether the person was engaged in some form of self-stimulation or a frantic effort to attain an exalted spiritual state.

Meanwhile, the audience engaged in a variety of brain-fulfillment activities, each person grasping at different controls. This produced a wave of intense, even frenzied spiritual climax that washed across the room. It was too much for Harris. His nervous system, already taxed, pulled to the brink of the dreaded neuronomy. Fortunately, when he collapsed, Amrake was able to grab his shirt and soften the fall.

Harris awoke to find himself in his own bed. He felt reasonably well, though quite fatigued. His scalp was a bit tense. Through the doorway of the bedroom, he saw Humboldt-Weizmann at the bar, still in her red garment, preparing something slowly and methodically. She was talking quietly into her datapad. Harris watched her until she gingerly entered the bedroom, holding a hot decompression brew.

"Well, Mr. Heliovision, how are we doing?" she asked.

It was strange for Harris to see his distinguished colleague in such intimate surroundings, forced though they were by the circumstances. Her face seemed as wooden as ever. She was not much older than himself but seemed much more worn.

"You had us worried, we thought it might be a neuronomy. But we summoned a physician, and it was just a case of cerebral disjunction. So we brought you here. Jason and the boss had to stay at the picnic, you know, politics and all that."

He confessed to her that the spectacle at the Nice estate was more than a "country wart" like him could absorb the very first time. Humboldt-Weizmann smiled, looking rather amused.

The two cyberscientists profited from the circumstances to broaden their acquaintance. Humboldt-Weizmann related that she, like Harris, had grown up in the region that would later become WestTech, on the Coast. Her parents, both senior researchers, moved in the highest scientific circles. After the Division, with Humboldt-Weizmann about to finish university, they secured important posts in the nascent CityTech, moving there as soon as it was built. It was as blue-blooded a story as one could imagine.

Harris, for his part, recounted some of the highlights of his odyssey from InterFun to BrainHost. Aside from mentioning that he lived his whole life in WestTech, he offered no biographical details antecedent to his employment at InterFun.

The conversation turned to the events at the Dome. Harris listened as intently as a seven year-old child listens to a ghost story. Humboldt-Weizmann recounted that Nice, who retired at age fifty after amassing untold wealth, turned his attention to improving the lot of his fellow human beings. He provided most of the seed money for the AntiStress Institute, attracting some of the sharpest minds in the TransTech world, not least of which was a young instructor at the WestTech Academy and former savior of InterFun, Chang Sun. After two months at the Institute, Sun had invented the Sander motion.

For a fleeting moment, Harris wondered what it would be like to perform the Sander motion with Humboldt-Weizmann, but instantly rejected the idea because of his physical repulsion from her.

The research, she explained, was a key pillar of a broader effort to ameliorate society's ills. There was a consensus among the CityTech intelligentsia that the tensions associated with the human mating ritual were wreaking havoc with people's lives, preventing true self-realization from occurring. Humboldt-Weizmann cited a recent study by the School of Advanced Inquiry revealing that on average, adults spend over seventy percent of their waking hours engaged in calculation, fantasy, regret, or some other counter-productive activity related to this area of human life.

After humans are liberated from the yoke of their mating ritual, the next step is to bestow upon them the means to achieve total self-realization. This would be achieved via activities such as the ones Harris saw when he first entered the main hall of the Nice estate. In fact, the estate was conceived, a priori, as a model of the perfect life, with the various stages of correct spiritual development actually mapped into the architecture.

All of this, however, was insufficient. It was William Nice's deep conviction that applied science alone could not solve humanity's dilemmas. It needed a spiritual dimension to drive the implementation phase. "And this," said Humboldt-Weizmann after taking a deep breath, "brings us to the Dome of Ascent." It was here that the two aspects of perfection—liberation and self-realization—meet. It was here that a hand-picked group would blaze the trail for others to follow, uniting the physical and spiritual aspects of the new path. Eventually, the entire world would unite in a single harmonious mass.

Harris looked like a person who had just been cured by a television preacher. He sat up straight in bed, his face pulled forward by enthusiasm. "What about the person lying on the platform?" he asked.

"So," said Humboldt-Weizmann, "you're wondering about the embracer." She lowered her eyes as the corners of her mouth contracted, giving the impression that she was guarding a secret. "That is not a simple matter. You may have noticed that its body looks much different than ours. When you feel a bit better, we'll go to a bar and I'll tell you about it over a hot swiffer. Okay?"

"Okay," said Harris. He felt ready at that very moment, but was reluctant to push the issue. And maybe she was right, that it was better to regain full strength before moving to the next stage. Clearly, what Humboldt-Weizmann was going to reveal was not a subject for light conversation.

He thanked her for her help. She wished him a speedy recovery, and departed.

Before falling asleep, Harris pondered the Dome of Ascent. It seemed like a logical extension of his acculturation in CityTech, another apprenticeship on the road to full absorption in BrainHost's top command. The obvious course of action would be to forge ahead, to educate himself systematically about the Dome and its ceremonies, as he had done with the coital matrix. Yet he was nagged by a sober assessment of his neurophysical limitations. Another outburst like the one at the Dome might very well push him into the abyss. He was overcome with melancholy: Should he simply insist on leading the heliovision research effort, and leave it at that, limiting his extracurricular activities to a reasonable but minimal level?

Harris was far from a resolution of the issue when he fell into a deep slumber.

Shortly after five o'clock the next morning, he woke up in a fog. Thoughts were spinning in his head, with no clear order or sense. His mind lurched from Humboldt-Weizmann to the Dome to the embracer to his old office at InterFun. Harris sat at the bar, elbows on the counter and holding his head, as if to halt the rush of images in his brain. He eventually managed to calm himself, concentrating on the workday ahead and the various tasks he needed to accomplish. As for the Dome and his failure there, he promised himself that he would shelve the topic until he had the chance to gather more information from Humboldt-Weizmann. Thereafter, he would devise a strategy for "getting back in the saddle."

That day at work, the cyberengineer would have to confront an entirely different challenge, one that was entirely beyond his control. Shortly after arriving at the office, he was perched over the computer, perusing material on the chemical composition of brain cells. His field of vision was rudely intruded by a summons to appear immediately at Bullock's office for an urgent conference with BrainHost's chief of security, known as "Mr. J." Harris wasted no time, stepping through the jaws of the furry pig and into the labyrinth, which after multiple twists and turns disgorged him into the chambers of the CEO.

"Thank you for coming right down, Harris," said the frosted countenance. "There's a problem you need to be aware of. Please sit down."

Harris noticed a twitch in Bullock's neck, a sure sign that something was awry.

"I'm afraid there's been a security breach. Several people's lives are in danger. I'm one of them, and so are you. I have to leave right now, but Mr. J. will give you the details." The CEO exited the room.

Mr. J. was a soft-spoken man in his late fifties, balding, fairly short and stocky, and quite inconspicuous looking. He was rumored to have played a key role in the great purging of outerwarts after the Division. Harris had met him only once at an initial briefing just after his arrival at the company, and had found him intimidating, but felt reassured that such a person was in charge of his safety.

"I can't give you too many details," said Mr. J., "but suffice it to say that there's a mole in BrainHost. Someone—and we believe it's at a senior level—is passing information to elements across the Line."

Harris was astonished at the security chief's matter-of-fact approach, simply presenting the situation, without a trace of excitement or anger.

"There's an off-chance of an assassination attempt, and I'm afraid that you're on the list. This group is focusing its efforts on stopping certain projects, especially heliovision."

"What is this group called?"

"You can obtain all the information you want by doing a search for an organization called the Root. Be sure to specify security level A-3 when you log in. You already have the necessary clearance. These outerwarts believe that the TransTech world is an unmitigated evil that must be destroyed at all costs."

Harris rubbed the back of his neck.

"Sorry to bring you all the bad news. I know you didn't bargain for this when you came on board. But we'll get through it. Everyone just needs to be a little more aware than usual, with a bit less consumption of pharmaceutical products."

Mr. J. accompanied Harris most of the way back to his office, then slipped into a small, inconspicuous portal marked by a simple yellow light instead of a hologram.

Newly parked at the computer, Harris set himself to the task at hand. Security level A-3 was set; the torrent of information poured in. Harris was shocked and distressed by what he read. Over the previous seven years, the Root had been true to its raison d'être, engaging in activity aimed at the total disruption of the TransTech world in general, and cyberbiological research in particular. A prime target was CloneFarm. Harris finally learned, by virtue of his new security classification, the real reason for the sudden death of the furry pig embryos. The Root's responsibility for the incident had never been revealed to the public.

The Root had always claimed adherents among the outerwarts, but recently they were making inroads within the TransTech world itself. Harris became privy to another secret: the truth concerning the arrest of Jonathan Handler-Stevenson, a top aide to the mayor of CityTech, the day after Harris arrived. The public had been told that Handler-Stevenson was taken into custody on the charge of attempted murder. But in reality, the authorities discovered that he had been coordinating the Root's efforts in CityTech for nearly a year. Among other mischief, it was believed that he was personally responsible for a fire at the Nice estate that caused severe damage and took the life of one of the gardeners.

Harris recoiled in his chair, nervously pressing his hand against the top of his head. His arm, in a reflexive movement, brought cephanil juice to his mouth, an action that gradually eased the knot in his chest. Life, rather abruptly, had become complicated. A few hours before, Harris's greatest concerns were his ability to perform a Sander motion or to understand ecstatic rituals. Now, his survival could no longer be taken for granted.

Doubt and conjecture ricocheted across his cerebrum. On the one hand, he reasoned, the briefing with Mr. J. could have been a simple precautionary measure. On the other hand, perhaps the danger was even greater, and the CEO and security chief were not divulging its full extent so as not to spread panic in the ranks. Past incidents, after all, had been kept secret. It was time, thought Harris, to have that conversation with Humboldt-Weizmann.

She accepted his invitation for drinks after work at the Sidewalk Café.

"Yes," sighed Humboldt-Weizmann, sipping her swiffer lite, "I'm afraid it's the truth. No, we're not on the verge of some grand takeover by the Root or anyone else. But they're quite capable of serious mayhem, the occasional murder or what have you." The what-have-you reverberated in Harris's skull as he scooped up a fistful of bunga nuts.

Humboldt-Weizmann could read the look of incredulity on her colleague's face. "Harris, let me tell you about the Dome. It will clarify the other issues as well." She wore a particularly serious face as she began her remarks. "That human being you saw there is the culmination of years of work."

Harris took a deep breath and glanced at the waterfall on the far side of the concourse. It was an impeccable display of the finest CityTech design. What better setting, he thought, to hear confidential information about state-of-the-art cyberbiological technology and its mortal enemies.

The R&D chief went on. "That special person was part of a select group of volunteers who underwent eighteen months of intensive treatment, most of it at CloneFarm. I was on the interdisciplinary steering committee that oversaw the project, code-named OvaTest. In view of the monumental significance of the endeavor for all of humanity, and in order to attract scientists from across the TransTech world, BrainHost, CloneFarm, and the other institutions involved pledged to make the research findings freely available to the entire scientific community.

"The goal of OvaTest was to produce a self-contained bisexual being, a sort of super-hermaphrodite. This individual, endowed with male and female organs, would experience a veritable blend of the two sexes' feelings, resulting in the epitome of sexual pleasure. A way had been found—combining surgery, brain fulfillment, and behavioral conditioning—to internally channel sexual arousal, so that the two sets of organs (plus their complementary glands and hormones) feed each other, as it were. There is no longer any limit to the level of ecstasy attained; it depends entirely on the person's capacity for fantasy. In other words, any fantasy involving human sexuality is immediately realized in the corresponding physical sensation.

"A critical component is the enhancement of the mind-genital link. Currently, several methods are being tried, such as certain cyberbiological products with which you are familiar. Other recipes are more traditional, drawing upon the vast historical reservoir of occult forces depicted in the frieze near the top of the Dome. William Nice has been experimenting rather adroitly with ancient methods, including some recently discovered Egyptian magic. But a certain plateau has been reached. In order to progress, there is a need for heliovision. Heliovision, with its exponential expansion of the liberation-realization nexus, will tear asunder the last obstacles in the way of unbridled, absolute fantasy. Thus the importance assigned to the project by BrainHost." She leaned back in her chair.

"Isn't it true," said Harris, "that the perfection of OvaTest will render the coital matrix obsolete?"

"That's an astute observation," noted Humboldt-Weizmann. "But it will still be several years before all this becomes available to the general public. In the meantime, the coital matrix is a good stepping-stone."

She and Harris concluded their meeting, and began a leisurely stroll back to the hypercush port. While discussing the architecture and other sights, they witnessed a phenomenon that Harris had never seen: A middle-aged man, dressed in a business suit, was being wheeled along in a baby carriage. Harris did a double-take. Was the man paralyzed, or in some other dire straits? Yet that *was,* he thought, a baby carriage. His glance met that of Humboldt-Weizmann's, who immediately understood her colleague's bewilderment.

"I suppose you don't have that yet in WestTech. It's one of the most exciting developments in CityTech life," she said, with an unusual note of enthusiasm in her voice.

Harris wasn't sure if she was joking, so he nodded in a neutral fashion.

"It's called the sabbatical cradle. It's for high-level warts whose stress has passed intolerable levels. But the treatment is still hard to get. You need an order signed by three physicians, one of whom must be a specialist in regression therapy."

Harris remained silent, looking at the R&D chief with rapt anticipation. Their march had slowed almost to a halt.

"What happens is this: The patient takes a sabbatical, and I mean a total one. They are relieved of all responsibility, gradually entering a state of complete relaxation. During the day, they are kept in a cradle, and transported in the carriage you saw. They sleep in a simulated womb. They breast-feed. Under his business suit, that individual was wearing diapers. He need not even control his bowels. It's absolutely brilliant. The sabbatical cradle was developed by the Caregiving department at the AntiStress Institute."

Harris was in awe. It did take some getting used to, he thought, but that was precisely because the idea was so bold. Once again, CityTech at the forefront. He felt joy at being a part of it all. How many people in WestTech, he sneered to himself, even heard of the sabbatical cradle?

The two senior cyberwarts parted company. On his way home, Harris reflected on his own performance, as it were, during the meeting with Humboldt-Weizmann. He was amazed at himself: for the first time, he had remained completely calm. Some threshold must have been reached, where things become self-evident, where one grasps the overarching significance of events, losing one's own sense of peril in the whirlwind of the communal experience. He grasped the import of his participation in the most dynamic scientific and social developments of the day.

The risk, he reasoned, was worth it. How many cyberwarts would not trade everything they owned for the opportunity he had received? He cocked his head back, basking in his accomplishment. Never was the word meteoric more appropriate. How quickly he had risen from bureaucratic drudgery to the cutting edge, from obscure project manager to trendsetter. His life was somewhat in danger, but what of it? Would he rather be back with Mandrake and the rest of the scoundrels at InterFun, vagabonding about aimlessly with Lincoln on the weekends? Such was a futile existence. No, thought Harris, there was no turning back. His placid reaction to Humboldt-Weizmann's story, this new flood of self-confidence, was the springboard from which he would plunge, mightily and irrevocably, into the new role that life had set before him.

In the weeks that followed, he settled into a routine. His orientation period at work was complete, his dwelling was arranged and configured to his liking, and he had his favorite restaurants and places of leisure. Tuesday nights he spent with Templeton. The conversation was dull, and by mutual consent was kept brief. The chat segment was followed by brain fulfillment and the coital matrix. The average one hour and fourteen minutes spent together (Harris calculated it) was, on the whole, an excellent way to alleviate tension and forget the daily grind.

Another milestone was reached when Harris was asked by ACE (the Association of Cyberbiological Engineers) to deliver a lecture at its upcoming annual meeting. BrainHost's heliovision effort was still a closely-guarded secret, but Humboldt-Weizmann, herself a former ACE CityTech chapter president, suggested to the association's board that Harris discuss some key issues involved in the race to finish the Triple M. He spent several long evenings preparing his remarks, in which he boasted of BrainHost's trailblazing efforts in this domain. He relished the prospect of addressing such an esteemed forum, although he knew that people from InterFun might be present. There had been no contact with his former colleagues since his abrupt departure.

The conference opened with introductory remarks by the president of ACE, Professor Benedict Hempelkraut. He lauded the "vast progress" made over the past year in the field of cyberbiology, both theoretical and applied. Hempelkraut then reviewed the program, spending a bit more time on his summary of Harris's session than on the others.

Harris, seated at the dais with the other speakers, looked around the room. It was a who's who of the field. The majority of the participants were from CityTech, with a smattering from institutions and commercial establishments elsewhere in the TransTech world. He recognized many of the faces, made famous by their appearance in the professional literature. There was no one, apparently, from WestTech, he noted with great relief. A logical occurrence, he reasoned, being that the region was merely a subcontracting backwater.

The atmosphere was loaded with anticipation. Harris was certain that the proceedings taking place at the conference would help set the agenda of the world's cyberbiological progress for the foreseeable future. This was the cutting edge—no more, no less.

It was in the men's room, just after lunch, that Beecely cornered him. Leaning in the doorway, arms folded and face scowling, he was watching Harris wash his hands. "How are we today, my little traitor-wart in a boss suit?" he asked.

Harris displayed a deadpan face, determined to ride out the encounter with a minimum of energy expended. Beecely advanced a step closer. There was no way for Harris to comfortably pass his adversary on the way to the door. He was pondering his limited options when Amrake entered the scene.

"Hey, if it isn't Beecely! I didn't know they let washed-up, third-rate bureaucrats into the conference. The Association must be hurting for cash these days." Up to that moment, Harris had respected Amrake, but now he felt his first real sensation of fondness toward the cyberwart. Beecely contorted his mouth in a show of disgust. "Tell your new colleague that everybody in WestTech knows what he did. And they're looking for him."

"I don't have to tell him," said Amrake, his entire face arched upward in a grin. "He's right here. But you're forgetting one thing, my dear WestTecher. You're in CityTech. Which makes you just another bunga nut on our plate." He motioned for Harris to leave, and the two citywarts left Beecely to fume silently, alone among the fixtures.

During the remainder of the conference, Harris watched for Beecely at every turn. The latter had departed, however, just after the scene in the men's room. Over the next few days, Harris and Amrake shared several good laughs as the two impersonated and otherwise ridiculed Beecely.

Amrake's personal life remained a mystery to Harris, as it was to many others. Like Bullock, he showed up everywhere, but always alone. And though he was present, he never participated fully. Humboldt-Weizmann had complained once that "Jason always comes with us to the Dome, but then finds some excuse to leave, like an urgent meeting or he forgot something." This remark reminded Harris of the evening at the Hyperclub just after his arrival in CityTech, when Amrake departed so abruptly. Various plans they had made together—even for lunch at work—always ended in a last-minute cancellation. Come to think of it, thought Harris, what exactly was Amrake's job? Even his title was vague: Senior Consultant for Corporate Strategy. Obviously, he held an important post, and was very close to the CEO. He was visible everywhere. No major decision at BrainHost was taken without his presence.

Whenever Harris pondered the mystery, or became annoyed after a cancellation, his thoughts eventually turned to Amrake's charismatic side. There was something frightfully compelling about the citywart's demeanor: always in good cheer, always encouraging. He never had anything but praise for Harris, and did everything possible to facilitate the WestTecher's absorption into his new environment.

One day, he caught Amrake in the cafeteria at an off hour, just as he was sitting down to eat a meal. Harris joined him across the table, and immediately decided to exploit the unexpected turn of events.

"Jason," he began. "can I ask you something?"

"Fire away, old boy," said Amrake, cutting into his deviralized alfalfa quiche.

"How did you locate Templeton? I mean, how did you...well..."

"...know that she was perfect for you?"

"Yes."

"I'll tell you. When we were planning the Jeptathia operation, I came across the dossier from that old CloakMaker project you were in, years ago. By the time I got through with that, I knew more about you than your own mother." Amrake wiped away a piece of alfalfa that had stuck to his chin.

"And I suppose," said Harris, "that's how you could preset my coordinates in the sidescope, and in the hypercush..."

"Nah, that kind of basic data is the easiest thing to get, when you have our level of security clearance. I'll show you how to do it sometime."

"Also, I wanted to know..."

Amrake abruptly stood up, looking at his watch. "Damn. I forgot about that meeting with the Board committee. Sorry about that. See you later."

Flustered by the departure, Harris quietly returned to his breaded maple-leaf tart. He resolved to "ambush" his mentor again, at the next opportunity.

That evening, Harris was set to receive his weekly session of muscular relaxation. Templeton, as always, showed up at the appointed time. She entered, greeted her partner, and then took her usual spot at the bar. All seemed normal, save the slightly concerned look on the dietician's face. Harris perceived it; the explanation did not tarry.

"Listen," came the monotone voice, accompanied by a downturn of the mouth and a swift one-quarter twist of the torso. "I want to stop our meetings."

Harris calmly asked for more details. He knew this would happen, having been unable to conceal his growing boredom during the previous two sessions.

"I don't think we can go any further in the matrix."

Harris at this point was staring vacantly into the middle of the room, his mind racing ahead to the action he would take the very next day to replace her. Three minutes later, Angela Templeton was on the far side of the door, much to their mutual relief.

Later that week, a key milestone arrived: Harris was to participate fully in a session at the Dome of Ascent. Bullock had been opposed, but Humboldt-Weizmann pleaded the case convincingly. Harris, she argued, had made great strides in the weeks since his inopportune collapse. Perhaps they had been hasty in bringing him there so soon after his arrival in the world's capital. In the interim, she and Harris had had several extended conversations on the subject, and he demonstrated great seriousness, enthusiasm, and depth of understanding. There was no question in her mind that he was ready.

Accompanied after work by Humboldt-Weizmann, Harris was greeted at the sanctuary by William Nice himself. The spiritual leader was tall and thin, but with a broad frame, giving him an imposing presence. The impression was amplified by his flowing, solid black robe, and a full head of long white hair that rested on his shoulders. The face had a day's worth of stubble. This was in harmony with Nice's slightly dark complexion and aquiline nose, which gave him the air of a poor yet noble Greek peasant. His beady eyes possessed an intense stare, which, combined with his excessively broad smile, could disarm any naysayer. In short, Nice looked like the prophet descending from the mountain.

Harris was able to exchange only a couple of words with Nice before the latter rushed off to his pulpit. Humboldt-Weizmann led Harris to a dressing room where they donned their blood robes, and then proceeded to the prep room to consume, together with a number of fellow devotees, various relaxants and brain-fulfillment substances. The atmosphere was solemn and purposeful. One had the unmistakable impression that something extraordinary was about to take place. By the time Harris was led into the main chamber, his head felt gelled and disconnected, as it were, from his neck and spine. But this time around, there was a difference: the CityTech meteor was in control, in tune with his sensations. He no longer fought them, was no longer intimidated by them. As he marched up to his seat, Harris had to restrain a smirk of self-satisfaction. Total calm prevailed, as reflected in a glance of understanding he exchanged with Humboldt-Weizmann.

The experience could only be described as expansive and uplifting beyond the furthest extent of his imagination. Explosive waves of liberating energy washed across the chamber as the ecstasy of the wildly contorting being on the platform was communicated to the participants via electric impulses. Nice was excellent as conductor of the festivities. His special touch for the evening was a narrated hexaflash projection, shown individually at each person's control panel, depicting in multidimensional realism an Eastern rite of self-immolation.

Harris was at the peak of his existence: All fear, regret, pain, and anxiety were purged from his system, along with a premonition that they would never return. His mind opened like the parting of the Red Sea, allowing him to burst through the psychological obstructions that his life had piled before him. He looked up at the historical frieze, and grasped its true message. He glimpsed what privileged pioneers throughout the generations had seen before him: the depths of power and liberation that lie beyond the simple material life.

The event ended with a respite in the prep room. The light was subdued and soothing music was being piped in. Silk mattresses and cushions dotted the floor. Harris parked his drained body on one of the cushions, and was promptly served a cool, refreshing drink. Hushed conversation filled the room, but it was followed by absolute silence when Nice made his entrance, accompanied by the embracer. The master whispered to it, gesturing in Harris's direction. The embracer slowly made its way to the adjoining cushion. Harris eyed it with great curiosity. Here, after all, was the physical manifestation of the philosophy that engendered the Dome and its ancillary phenomena.

Even for the "new" Harris, the sight of the androgynous creature was taxing. It was thin, naked, and hairless, with pale and milky skin, almost corpse-like. The thin frame could be classified as neither male nor female, being absolutely nondescript. Similarly, the facial features were dull and non-obtrusive, giving the head the appearance of a ball. The breasts were flat and lacked nipples; the only sign of their erstwhile existence was a circle of slightly darker pigmentation across an area about half an inch in diameter. Likewise, the genital area was smooth, excepting a tiny protuberance of the pubic bone.

The embracer sat down with a stiff but effortless motion. It rotated its bland face toward the cyberengineer. The mouth opened just a crack, while the other features displayed no movement. Its eyes were glassy and without depth, like those of a fish. Harris braced for the words that would surely arrive.

"Thank you for coming," said the creature, in a soothing and faintly feminine voice. "Please don't be alarmed by my appearance. Deep down, I'm just a cyberwart like you, except that I was given a wonderful opportunity to change my life. I hope we can be friends."

Harris cleared his throat, sat up straight, and nodded.

"Sorry," it continued, "I have to go now. Mr. Nice is waiting for me. But I'm sure we'll meet again soon." It moved rapidly toward its mentor.

Harris craved a return to the placid state he had experienced just a few minutes before. The desire could not be satisfied at that moment. His nervous system had been jarred, and required a certain time to readjust. It was only several minutes later that he felt his calm, confident composure begin to return. He stretched out on one of the mattresses, closed his eyes, listened to the hushed conversation, and let his mind wander back to the delicious stimuli of the Dome.

The next day at work, Harris pondered the steps necessary to replace his weekly relaxation partner. He reached the conclusion that it might not be necessary to replace her immediately. Maybe it was time for a new strategy. He recalled Humboldt-Weizmann's remark that the coital matrix was only a stepping-stone on the way to the total fulfillment of OvaTest. Perhaps, he mused, there was an additional stepping-stone between the two, an interim stage between the coital matrix and embracerhood. He knew that some time would pass before he was ready for the latter, yet he felt the urge to match his spiritual advancement on the physical plane as well. He envisaged the interim stage as a supercharged Dome experience, combined with an early, unauthorized version of heliovision.

This new personal game plan provided a powerful impetus for his work. It was soon noticed around BrainHost that Harris had become a beacon of inspiration, a model employee for all to emulate. New expressions were heard, such as "to finish that task on time, you need to pull a Harris," or "even Harris couldn't organize something like that." No one knew that behind this changed behavior was the drive to experience a unique, heretofore untested form of the realization-liberation nexus.

PART TWO

CHAPTER FIVE

▼

At the very moment that Harris laid his eyes upon the embracer, Judge Ebenezer Forrester was presiding over a jury of outerwarts that had convened in solemn assembly to try one Thaddeus Jones. Jones was on trial in Jeptathia's Supreme Court for the crime of stealing and selling intellectual property. This, in any event, was the formal charge. His real offense was that he passed critical technological information to elements in the TransTech world—information that was vital to the Triple M research effort. In doing so, he violated one of the strictest of all outerwart taboos: helping the cyberwarts advance their social agenda.

Jones hung his head in shame. He had been an eminently respectable member of the community, a father and grandfather. It was not known what had motivated him to gamble it all away for a crass material benefit. His family and closest associates were humiliated.

To Forrester, who had been acquainted with Jones since well before the Division, the mystery was particularly onerous. The emotional burden of the case was amplified by the tenor of events in Forrester's own life. The outerwart judge was pushing sixty; a mild stroke several years earlier had left him with a slight limp and a heaviness of the mouth that caused an occasional slurred word. He was overweight and always somewhat unkempt.

He regretted giving his consent to adjudicate in the Jones affair, though he rose to the challenge, doing his best under difficult circumstances. He was a quiet, private sort, always shying away from publicity. It was by virtue of his great stature in the community as physician and scholar that he had been nominated to the post.

The judge glanced across the dank, dimly-lit chamber. The tables and benches were creaking from age, and the off-white ceiling and walls were moldy and peeling. The people looked dusty and yellowed, like old documents taken out of cartons after many years of storage. It was a pitiful sight, and it tightened the vise on Forrester's already broken heart. The final arguments in the case had just been heard. He had to summon some new energy just to lift and bang the gavel, announcing a recess until the following day.

Forrester began his two-mile trek home on foot, cracked leather briefcase in hand. The hike gave him ample time to engage in one of his favorite pursuits: deep reflection on his life and his society. As he looked at the dilapidated structures of the vast shanty town, he was reminded of the constant deterioration of Jeptathia, and indeed, of any piece of outerwart territory with which he was familiar. And there seemed to be no end in sight. The best and the brightest on his side of the Line were disappearing, either through apathy and withdrawal, or defection to the TransTech world. To make matters worse, violations of outerwart sovereignty were common, with new TransTech enclaves appearing at an alarming rate.

If the rumors about the latest research in CityTech were true—if an advanced hermaphrodite was being hatched—he might as well throw in the towel. These developments could sound the death knell for any resistance. Even the Root underground organization, he thought, was in the final analysis just a gang of hotheads. They had no sophistication and were incapable of real leadership. His brief encounters with the group's top command, some of whom he had known since childhood, ended consistently in disappointment and chagrin.

Forrester reached his destination, out of breath and sticky from sweat. His home was comfortable by Jeptathia standards. Most dwellings in the ramshackle urban agglomeration were nothing more than rat-infested hovels. The Forresters inhabited a three-room apartment in a building with a dozen or so units, structurally sound and hygienic, but barely. There was even a tiny yard, or, more precisely, a ten-foot wide strip of dirt between the building and its fence. The bland exterior stucco had been replastered in so many spots that it more closely resembled a quilt than a wall.

Slipping the key into the door, he released his customary sigh. He stopped momentarily, as the image of Jones's shamed head entered his thoughts. A knot of sadness gripped his heart, leaving him immobile for several seconds. He was aroused from his reverie by the gentle sound of his wife's voice, inquiring as to whether he intended to come into the flat. He grunted something under his breath, opened the door, and stepped inside.

Forrester looked into his wife's eyes, which were alight with compassion and concern. Jessica Forrester was the last of a breed. At the time of the Division, she had already been a mother of two, and one of the country's leading authorities on ancient Greek literature. Despite everything, she had aged well, and still preserved an inner warmth that radiated across her face. Her strong, well-carved features announced tenaciousness and a zest for life. One would not pick her out in a crowd as one of the most attractive women, but after several minutes in her presence, her beauty crept up and seized the beholder.

Forrester kissed his wife, and plummeted into an old, ragged leather armchair. He had lately acquired a nearly continual frown. Most of his friends had either died, disappeared, or lapsed into chronic and extreme apathy. The family's resources had dwindled down to almost nothing. And it seemed, in light of current events, that it was only a matter of time before he himself would "disappear" as well.

As he watched his wife closing the curtains, the physician thought back to earlier days. When the Division had occurred, the prestigious hospital at which he worked found itself on the wrong side of the Line. The senior staff dispersed to the four corners of the earth. Forrester managed to hang on for several years, until he was offered a plum position at the newly-formed CityTech Medical Center. He accepted, though he and Jessica entertained grave misgivings regarding the direction of the new society. Soon after assuming his duties at the medical center, he was faced with a dilemma. The center's management unveiled a new project, with Forrester at the helm: Find a way, via manipulation of the brain, to disengage the human sexual drive and replace it with an alternative attraction.

His immediate and unnuanced refusal to cooperate set in motion a five-month odyssey for the Forresters. They migrated from pillar to post, seeking refuge among friends and former associates. They ended up in Jeptathia, the decaying relic of a once affluent and thriving city. The couple banded together with assorted misfits and adventurers to splice together a workable life. Forrester became the neighborhood physician, while his spouse—formerly a tenured professor of the classics—organized the city's only school with Greek and Latin in the curriculum. Later, Forrester went to work at Jeptathia General Hospital, heading up its department of neurology, eventually becoming the hospital's overall chief of surgery. He was currently retired, devoting his time to writing and to treating a small number of special patients.

Jessica sat down on the sofa next to her husband, looking solemn.

"What is it?" asked Forrester, becoming concerned.

With a trembling voice, she made the simple announcement: "There's a meeting tonight."

Forrester nodded and sighed, as he knew it would come to this. Normal life was about to end; chaos was waiting at the gates. For years he had dreaded this moment. But at present it seemed to be a natural and inexorable fate, irresistible in its force.

"It's the meeting we talked about last week," explained Jessica. "They're coming to pick you up at around eight o'clock. I said that you'd be ready, unless they hear from us otherwise."

She sat on the stool next to her husband, and rested her head on his lap. He stroked her hair and gently massaged her neck, as he often did. His thoughts wandered to their two children. One, a girl, died as a teenager in a hiking accident. The other child, a boy, defected some two years previously, with his wife and newborn baby, to a faraway sector of the TransTech world. Forrester stifled an impulse to torture himself by conjuring up vivid and painful memories. Instead, he pondered the evening's rendezvous, calculating his anticipated level of disappointment.

He was transported for over an hour by truck to what had been an underground security center for a nuclear research facility, abandoned and sealed before the Division. Some enterprising Root engineers had managed to locate and open the security center, and build a new access tunnel. The tunnel was about three hundred yards long, in four segments on varying levels, connected by spiral staircases. It took Forrester a good fifteen minutes to make his way from the tunnel entrance to the security center.

He surveyed the room. It was circular, about thirty feet across, with control panels around the periphery. Some of the buttons, lights, and levers were still in place, interspersed with gaping holes where computers and other machines had been removed. In the middle of the former high-tech showcase were several tattered wooden chairs and benches, and a peeling Formica-topped table taken from an adjoining room. Forrester found the contrast of erstwhile glory and actual shabbiness to be eerie and oppressive.

His heart sank even further as he took stock of the other attendees, and listened to their conversations. They matched precisely his expectations: Intelligent individuals with the best of intentions, who clearly perceived the threat posed by the TransTech world, yet had little or no grasp of the arts of war, politics, or propaganda. The entire undertaking, he reckoned, was doomed to failure. It was, however, the only game in town.

A rough-looking man in his late forties moved to the front of the room and called the meeting to order. Forrester recognized him as Carl Ingerman, commander-in-chief of the Root. They had met some years earlier at the home of a mutual friend. Then, as now, he considered the rebel leader to be a rather odd sort. This impression was undoubtedly reinforced by a rare respiratory disorder that caused Ingerman to be constantly exhaling a chain of snorts.

Despite the misgivings, Forrester knew that Ingerman's integrity was airtight. Though not always a brilliant strategist, and not possessing an enormous reservoir of charisma, he had proven himself to be a courageous and daring warrior. The chief always led his troops into battle, and never asked anyone to do something he would not do (and in most cases, had not done) himself. Moreover, since the day when he founded the Root with three other men—all subsequently killed in the line of duty—no one ever saw Ingerman take advantage of anyone. He was tough and demanding, but never abusive. And he never asked for any personal benefit by virtue of his position. Ingerman thus enjoyed the respect and loyalty of all Root personnel.

Ingerman had lived his entire life in Jeptathia, cradle of the Root. Most of the group's top command originated in the town, which before the Division had been a mecca for artists, writers, and assorted free-thinkers. At first, the TransTech elite was happy to wash its hands of the locale and its intelligentsia, letting it slowly rot. The rot proceeded apace; Jeptathia, however, spawned the movement that most threatened the peace and stability of the TransTech world.

In the months preceding the Division, the officer corps began to choose sides. Sometimes, entire bases declared their loyalty for one camp or the other. The outerwarts, as they came to be known, controlled many more personnel and bases than their adversaries, but rapidly lost control of the air force, the navy, and the weapons of mass destruction. Their fate was all but sealed.

From the outset, Ingerman chose the outerwart side, and made no attempt to conceal it. He had no taste whatsoever for the TransTech way of life. He helped organize the seizure of an army base, and later became the commander of outerwart forces in the battle for Jeptathia. Because the city had no strategic value, the new TransTech command sent in a secondary, predominantly female armored infantry unit to seize the town. They were trounced by Ingerman and his men. A more skilled and experienced unit was sent in. The fighting was fierce, with severe casualties on both sides. A stand-off ensued, with outerwart forces remaining in control of Jeptathia. The TransTech brass saw no further value in the siege of the city. Instead, they withdrew their forces to positions well away from the metropolitan area. So it remained until the overall cease-fire.

Presently, there were no introductory remarks and no social niceties. Ingerman reviewed, in a businesslike manner, several preliminary items, and then proceeded to the main topic. He described a daring operation that would take place in the heart of CityTech. A key individual would be kidnapped and brought back to outerwart territory. Through a combination of drugs and brainwashing, he would first be made to divulge certain information, and then be persuaded that the cause of the Root was just. Later, by means of a staged escape from captivity, he would be sent back to CityTech to become an agent for the Root. If for some reason there was fear of betrayal, he would be eliminated.

One of the younger operatives switched on an old-fashioned slide projector and dimmed the lights. Ingerman activated the remote-control device, and the projector flashed onto the wall a large photo of a person. "This is our man. Brand new in CityTech. Head of heliovision research at BrainHost. Fits the profile perfectly," summarized the insurgent leader.

He explained why Harris had been selected. The target was new in CityTech, recently imported from WestTech, where he had held an inconsequential junior position. His psychological profile indicated a lack of emotional stability, dependence on mood-altering substances, and a feeling of listlessness. He had demonstrated his lack of loyalty when presented with enticements. And his current endeavors in the domain of heliovision placed him at the forefront of the CityTech research effort.

Ingerman switched the slides, showing Harris on the hypercush platform at the TransTech enclave in Jeptathia. This was followed by additional photos taken at the time of the synchbox purchase from Thaddeus Jones. "As many of you know, it was this WestTech bureaucrat who made the deal with Jones. CityTech knew it was coming, so they shut down the power grid and sent someone in there to bribe him. They wrapped up the whole deal in a matter of hours, getting this guy to abandon his whole life. So we'll get a hold of him too. Take away his bunga nuts for a day and he'll abandon his own mother."

Ingerman outlined the parameters of the mission, code-named Operation Spearhead. Someone would be sent from Jeptathia to oversee the operation, making use of agents already in CityTech. This person would have to possess a scientific background, and be familiar with cyberbiology and related issues. The agent would observe Harris for a while, and then a decision would be made regarding the type of bait to be used. The entire mission would take three months, from the time the supervising agent departed from Jeptathia until the time Harris returned to CityTech as a Root sympathizer. The operatives taking part in Spearhead would be contacted separately within forty-eight hours.

The meeting was adjourned. Forrester, as was his custom, waited for most of the crowd to leave the room before getting up. He began his slow limp to the door, already feeling the onslaught of doubt and disappointment that descended upon his mind like vultures swarming onto carrion. He was intercepted by the commander, who gently guided him aside.

"We want you to lead the mission," declared Ingerman, in a somber tone of voice.

Forrester let out an audible sigh, and slowly backed into the nearest chair. The insurgent leader quickly took up position alongside. Forrester raised his head to see Ingerman's intense and calculating look, accompanied by a string of rapid-fire snorts. Forrester had pegged the likelihood of this occurrence at about seventy percent, thus surprise was not a factor. Looking at his new commander's face, he was overcome by melancholy. Does everything, he asked himself, boil down to this? Was it true—is this hyperventilating hothead really holding the reins, guiding our destiny? It was ludicrous and pathetic, he thought, but there was no choice. It's either go along, or fade into oblivion like so many others, fighting a futile war of attrition against apathy and despair. Forrester estimated his chances of surviving the mission at around ten percent.

He indicated his acceptance. It was agreed that he would join the other members of the Spearhead task force at an orientation briefing to be held at a different location two days later. "Welcome to the Root," snorted Ingerman.

During the truck ride home, Forrester pondered his fate. He indulged his self-pity, feeling like a dupe. But then it struck him: Why not? Life was barely livable now, what about in three years? In five? If he passed up this opportunity, he would never forgive himself. He could probably communicate effectively with this Harris chap, scientist to scientist. Forrester rejected Ingerman's facile characterization of him as a "bureaucrat." Heliovision was as complex as it was pernicious. A simple functionary does not become one of the world's leading experts in such a domain. And there could be multiple explanations for his abandonment of WestTech. In all probability, reasoned Forrester, this man has a logical side to his character. Perhaps he could be made to see the dangers inherent in the project. Unfortunately, there was no material benefit with which to entice him, having already arrived at the pinnacle of the planet's decadence. But maybe there was something he lacked. Finding it would require intensive research and observation.

The truck pulled up to Forrester's building. It was nearly 1:00 AM; the street was deserted. Exhausted, he lumbered up the stairs, and leaned on the door of the apartment for a minute to catch his breath. He opened it slowly and quietly, so as not to wake Jessica. He found her seated on the couch, awake but groggy, with an open book in her lap. It took her a couple of seconds to snap out of the drowsiness. When she did, she embraced her husband.

"How did it go?" she asked.

"It went well," replied Forrester. He had no intention of revealing his pessimistic appraisal of the Root. "Come, let's go to sleep."

"But wait," said Jessica, with a look of skepticism on her face. "Are you *sure* it went well?"

"As well as could be expected." He took her hand in his and led her to the bedroom.

Early the next morning, Forrester returned to the courthouse to wrap up deliberations on the fate of Thaddeus Jones. After some brief formalities, he sent the jury into an adjoining conference room to discuss the case and render a verdict. He pounded the gavel, announcing a recess until the end of jury deliberations.

Forrester asked the bailiff to escort the defendant into the judge's chamber. The officer brought Jones in, handcuffed him to the chair, and exited the room. There, alone with the accused, Forrester viewed the tragic picture of a broken man. Jones was an accomplished theoretical mathematician, his work cited in numerous journals. Like Forrester, he lived a fairly comfortable life by Jeptathia standards. If he had wanted to significantly upgrade his material existence, reasoned Forrester, he could have simply defected to the TransTech world. A host of commercial establishments would have jumped at the chance to hire him. So why risk everything with an illegal act?

"Why did you do it?" asked Forrester. "It's off the record. I just want to know. For myself."

Jones let his head fall onto the top of his chest as tears silently streamed down his face. It took a couple of minutes before he raised his head, wiped his face on his sleeve, and looked Forrester in the eye. "I wanted everything. I wanted to give more to my family, to get a house out in the country somewhere."

"But you knew what they would do with that information."

"I didn't know...I mean, I did know; I just don't know why." After a long pause, Jones looked up with the pathetic eyes of a dog who has been whipped. "I was losing my mind. I can't take it anymore, this crazy place. Look how many brilliant minds we have, and we're living in a junkyard."

Forrester sighed and shook his head. He called in the bailiff, and the prisoner was taken away.

The jury returned within half an hour. The verdict was guilty as charged. Forrester pronounced the mandatory minimum sentence, two years in prison, and pounded the gavel for the last time.

The Root orientation meeting for Operation Spearhead took place as planned. Forrester was picked up in an obscure part of town and transported to a small house in an outlying area. He met the people that were to be his new cohorts, most of them destined to play a supporting role from outerwart territory. They seemed unimpressive, to the say the least. As he greeted them one by one, Forrester asked himself how they had managed to place themselves in descending order of quality, going from bad to worse. The only exception was the last one on the list, an agent already living in CityTech, who would be his primary collaborator on the scene.

Forrester instantly recognized Marilyn Sommers. They had never met, but he had seen her picture in medical journals. Marilyn was head of the department of clinical psychology at CityTech Medical Center. A single woman in her mid thirties, she was as beautiful as she was accomplished: Slender, 5 foot 8, with silky blond hair that fell naturally onto her graceful shoulders. Her sparkling green eyes and petite nose completed the portrait of attractiveness.

Ingerman presented an overview of Operation Spearhead. Marilyn would announce to the medical center's management that she had been in contact with Forrester, who for some time—so goes the story—had been seeking a way to defect to CityTech. He would then formally apply to the medical center for permission to conduct the research he had so adamantly refused years before. Marilyn would assure the task force that there was a pressing need for someone to pursue serious work in this area, and that Forrester's name came up occasionally in conversation, along the lines of "too bad we blew that one."

No particular obstacles were foreseen. Defections by the outerwart elite (an act known in CityTech parlance as "understanding") were a daily occurrence. Most people would be surprised that Forrester held out as long as he did, and they might even be flattered that a scientist of such stature wanted to work at their institution, in pure research, when he could make much more money at a commercial outfit such as BrainHost.

With all arrangements concluded, Forrester would move to CityTech, alone, for a probationary period. He would "find" lodging in Browser Beach, in a secured apartment to be prepared by Marilyn and other operatives. After becoming sufficiently ensconced in his new research position, he would invent a pretext for contacting Harris. In the meantime, the two Root operatives would study and observe the cyberengineer, eventually formulating a strategy for the enticement. One possibility would be an assertion by Forrester that he knows of a key piece of information being developed by some rogue outerwarts who wanted to sell it, a transaction similar to Harris's purchase of the Triple M equations from Thaddeus Jones.

Without being explicit, Ingerman floated the idea of a seduction. Marilyn, remaining calm, said that she was willing to employ any method to ensure the success of the mission—as she had proven in the past—but that anyone who was familiar with the current "romantic" life of the CityTech elite knew that this option was likely to be a non-starter. Leaning toward Forrester, she whispered, "I'll explain all that to you later." Forrester knew of the coital matrix and related developments, but was unaware of the Dome and the influence it was having on Harris's lifestyle.

After the briefing, lunch was served in the dining room. The meal gave Marilyn and Forrester a chance to become better acquainted.

"When I was a teenager just before the Division," said Marilyn, "my mother, father, and brother were killed in the Bombardments."

"I'm really very sorry to hear that," said Forrester.

"Thank you. The area we lived in was destroyed by the TransTech forces. Later it was absorbed into the WestTech zone. I never forgave the architects of the attack, who went on to become key leaders of CityTech. As I completed my education and progressed in life, I swore that I would never internalize their customs and worldview, and that one day I would see justice be served. The chance to make a difference appeared when I made the acquaintance of Jonathan Handler-Stevenson, who brought me into the fold. And now, less than a year later, here I am in Spearhead."

Forrester learned that the psychologist was acquainted with Harris since her youth, being only one year younger and going to the same high school. In those days, they had met only a couple of times. Recently, they exchanged a few words when one evening they happened to be in the same restaurant in Browser Beach. In any case, she was perfectly familiar with Harris's background and basic mentality. This, combined with her seductive beauty, intelligence, experience in psychology, knowledge of CityTech, and indomitable hatred of the enemy, made her a formidable ally.

"By the way," he asked, "what do you tell your CityTech colleagues when you come here?"

"That I'm visiting my mother, who is supposedly deathly ill, at Jeptathia General Hospital. I stay at a hotel in the enclave, and go visit her several times over the course of my visit. One of our agents is actually occupying a hospital bed. She plays the part of Mom."

"Very clever."

Forrester had his own cover-up to consider. He was troubled by the damage that might be caused by his departure for CityTech. First, he would have to transfer responsibility for his patients during his absence. The larger issue that loomed, however, was how to prevent the impression of a defection to CityTech, an event that could demoralize a fairly wide swath of Jeptathia's higher professional circles. Forrester formulated a strategy: He would say that he had exhausted the research and treatment capabilities of Jeptathia. He wanted to develop cures and therapy for certain rare neurological disorders, and the work could be carried out only in CityTech. Of course, people might doubt his story if and when they discovered the exact nature of the research he was hired to conduct. But this was a risk that had to be taken. At least, he thought, it was mitigated by the expected short duration of Operation Spearhead.

His wife Jessica assisted him in explaining the move to friends and colleagues. She insisted on doing her part, despite Forrester's objections. He was saddened by the fact that she had to be involved in the disinformation campaign, justified though it was. What saddened him even more, however, was that Jessica expected the absence to be temporary whereas Forrester had little hope that he would complete the mission unscathed. Returning home and continuing his life as a free man seemed to be a highly improbable outcome.

Marilyn departed the next morning for the world's capital. During the week that followed, she spared no effort to accomplish the first goal of the mission. As a result of her activity, the medical center was soon buzzing with gossip about Forrester's imminent "understanding." Despite his earlier snub of the TransTech world, he was very much a respected figure in the profession. His leading role in the discovery of the cure for Parkinson's disease was only the most recent of his legendary achievements, and in far less than ideal conditions.

There was, however, an unexpected hitch. Apparently there was no "psychosocial oppression clause" under which Forrester could be hired by the medical center. As Marilyn explained to him, no person can be hired by a public institution in CityTech solely on the basis of his qualifications—with the sole exception of overwhelming public need, as validated by a unanimous vote of the High Court.

He did not have a Type R sexual orientation nor any history of trauma caused by genetic alteration. He was not the victim (at least not certified) of an exclusivist emotional redirection; that is, emotional damage caused by the rerouting of love and affection away from the aggrieved party, toward other undeserving individuals. It was only after intervention by the medical center's top management that Forrester was recognized by the relevant government authorities as "scarred and shamed" by the effects of his stroke, with the aggravated circumstance of being shunned by certain friends and colleagues as a result of his act of understanding. This entitled him to obtain the necessary classification.

Three weeks and one day after the start of Marilyn's lobbying campaign, Forrester was escorted from the CityTech air facility to the medical center. Top management had organized a reception to celebrate the signing of the contract, and to show off their latest catch to the medical and scientific community. As it turned out, the agreed-upon salary was fairly modest, but some attractive perks were thrown into the bargain: a signing bonus; an extended vacation after one year of service; and a private (though used) hypercush.

As Forrester pressed the flesh, he was astonished by the friendliness and openness of his new colleagues and others of their milieu. He had expected them to look down their noses at him. And that is indeed what had happened over the years, on the occasions that Forrester encountered one of his opposite number from the TransTech world. But things were very different when he was set to join them. It was as if they were greeting a relative returning home after a long absence.

At the forefront of Forrester's consciousness was a feeling of guilt. Few and far between were the times that he had been compelled to mislead another human being, almost always due to some force majeure. But at this very moment, he was deceiving hundreds—and, via the spread of information, thousands or even millions of people. The overall cause for which he was fighting, he reflected, was just and proper beyond the shadow of a doubt, but did that erase the impact of his lies on the individual level? And if this was merely at the outset, how would he feel at the moment of the grand betrayal, several weeks hence?

These thoughts, combined with the voyage from Jeptathia and the jolt of the radically different environment, finally took their toll on Forrester's ailing body. He felt faint; Marilyn had to escort him to an armchair at the side of the room. He indicated his desire to depart. His accomplice notified the necessary people on his behalf, and the two Root agents headed for the hypercush port.

Marilyn set the navizoom as Forrester wearily looked on. According to the instruments, the ride would take sixteen minutes and fifty-two seconds. One could see from his expression that the suffering was more emotional than physical. "I know how you feel," she said. "This really is a lousy business. If the world wasn't such a mess, you'd have some juicy top university chair, and you wouldn't have to deal with anything else."

Forrester thanked her. Then, after looking at the young woman's delicate face, he reasoned that, all things considered, the roles should be reversed. He was old enough to be her father. He had lived a full life, albeit under difficult conditions, but still had pursued a splendid career, raised a family—in short, carved an honest niche for himself in the world. But look at Marilyn: a young, attractive, intelligent woman, orphaned in her vulnerable adolescence, forced to assimilate into professional and social circles that were anathema to her. Even worse, he thought, once she established herself in those circles, it was all a mirage, a vast game of deception. So full of life, so caring and personable, she has no choice but to totally conceal her inner spirit from those around her.

He stared at her with a look of pity, thereby betraying his thoughts. She looked away, causing several minutes of awkward silence. Forrester could find nothing intelligent to say, so he concealed his embarrassment in a long sigh of fatigue. Marilyn watched the road, and the silence continued.

Chapter Six

▼

Forrester's perception was entirely accurate. Marilyn lived in a state of loneliness and despair. More often than not she cried herself to sleep, rolling around in bed, moaning from emotional anguish. On numerous occasions, she was tempted to imbibe or ingest one or another pharmaceutical product, but a stronger force overcame and crushed the desire. To partake would be tantamount to surrender. Ultimately, what sustained her was her incontrovertible opposition to the lifestyle and belief system of the TransTech world. It was an animosity that knew no limits.

But obstinacy had its cost. Marilyn had no real friends. She could at least feel some comfort in the presence of other Root agents, but contact was sporadic at best, and the nature of their work demanded a formalized code of behavior. Moreover, though united in their contempt for the TransTech world, their origins and temperament were often quite different.

She did, however, have some superficial "friendships," if only to maintain appearances. For example, Olivia Gardner, the manager of the lab at the medical center. The two women would go out occasionally for dinner or some light entertainment. Gardner was actually a rather pleasant sort, but totally in tune with the CityTech way of thinking. Marilyn endeavored to limit the conversations to innocuous topics. She feared that if she were to slip and reveal the most miniscule aspect of her true self, Gardner immediately would see through her cover.

This dissimulation was a constant feature of her life. It followed her everywhere, lurking in the background of every conversation, every contact. She was forced to adapt her facial expression, her tone of voice, her clothing, her fingernails, her posture—every aspect of her public persona was falsified.

One escape route from this incessant trap was Marilyn's job at the medical center. It provided a way to concentrate intensely without having to worry, much of the time, about the social trimmings. This device, however, was nearing the end of its life span. Although Marilyn was generally held in high esteem by her colleagues, she was out of step with the trends in her field. The classical therapeutic approaches, and indeed all of clinical psychology as it had been practiced for at least a century, were being tossed into the dustbin of history. The latest fashion across the TransTech world was a new school of thought called Expressionism. Its adherents firmly rejected the conclusions and methods of their predecessors.

The basic tenet of Expressionism is as follows: Every human being previously thought to be mentally handicapped is in reality completely normal and healthy; that is, emotionally and psychologically. The problems and frustrations experienced by "patients" are the result of social barriers to their personalized mode of expression. All individuals have their own unique form of expression, and they cannot be happy and well-adjusted until their surrounding environment recognizes and adapts to this specific requirement. Thus treatment is aimed at the public, not the individual.

Over the course of just two years, about one-third of the practitioners on Marilyn's staff had become full-fledged expressionists, with another third favorably predisposed. The confrontations were multiplying. There was the case of the man who worked as a janitor in a large dog and cat grooming salon in Deltoid. Several customers had complained to the boutique's management that their pets returned from their sojourn at the salon in an enervated, almost maniacal state. After a brief investigation, it was found that the janitor had lightly drugged the animals, and then tried to force them to mate with the other species.

The janitor was promptly arrested. The judge released him after reaching an agreement among all parties that the man would enter an intensive course of treatment at the CityTech Medical Center. The psychologist in charge of the treatment as well as the assisting intern were both sworn expressionists. The diagnosis: The salon had deprived the man of the opportunity to pursue his own unique form of self-expression, resulting in the controversial behavior. The prescribed treatment: The salon must redesign its environment to accommodate his needs. Apparently, his desire to radiate love and tenderness throughout the world was extremely strong. The salon could, for example, set up a special room where the janitor could kiss and cuddle the animals. This was in addition to monetary damages that would be paid to help compensate him for his suffering.

The proprietors of the salon, of course, were aghast at this turn of events, and flatly refused to cooperate. The attending psychologists, aided by sympathetic colleagues, decided to make this a test case. They responded to the salon's obstinacy by waging a no-holds-barred public relations campaign to humiliate and browbeat the owners. Marilyn finally convinced the director of the medical center to put an end to the campaign of the rogue psychologists. But she knew that in the not-so-distant future, she would be considered the rogue.

A brief escape from Marilyn's isolation was found in a romantic interlude that began in Jeptathia. Just after joining the Root, she spent three weeks in a general orientation program for new agents. To the people in CityTech, Marilyn claimed she was taking a vacation in an obscure exotic resort. She was provided with forged tickets, taxi receipts, photos, and souvenirs from the supposed destination. A young female Root sympathizer in the same locale checked into the hotel using her name.

At the training course there was a young man from WestTech, the male equivalent of Marilyn: brave, attractive, obsessive. The electricity flowed abundantly. There was hardly a moment when they could speak privately during the highly intensive program. But at the end of the course, the two agents agreed to keep in touch.

Just over a month after the program ended, the WestTech agent had occasion to visit CityTech on a business trip. The couple violated one of the cardinal rules of Root operating procedure by joining together in carnal union. The only reason the two highly-committed and professional agents could arrive at this behavior was that the process occurred with such ease, with such a natural flow of reciprocal energy.

The mutual attraction and need was total—anything less would have caused an insidious doubt, spoiling the progress from one stage to the next.

When the union took place, it was without bounds. A dam burst inside Marilyn, releasing a torrent of pent-up yearning. She was reunited with a deeply suppressed aspect of her soul, an act that involved the traversal of light-years of emotional and spiritual space.

The price was dear. For quite some time thereafter, the usual difficulties in Marilyn's life were amplified. Every illegitimate smile, every insincere gesture was a torture of the highest order. The young woman felt herself asphyxiated. Matters were made worse by the death of her lover just two weeks after his visit. He was killed by police during his first mission, an attempt to delete the database at his company, a major WestTech manufacturer of computer components. Marilyn's existence became a living death. She sought refuge in the Root, and boosted her activity level to the maximum allowed by the top command.

Presently, Browser Beach appeared on the navizoom. "Here we are," declared Marilyn. Forrester nodded his agreement, but his mind had drifted to an evaluation of his immediate surroundings. So this is a hypercush, he remarked to himself. There certainly is no shortage of hype about this invention. How many times did he have to listen to people recount, with starry eyes, the time they had seen (or for the select few, actually traveled in) one of these things. It was certainly efficient, but almost all the technology involved was child's play compared to even, say, pre-Division avionics or medical imaging equipment. Its potential for widespread application was close to nil, reasoned Forrester, requiring as it did substantial headways and sensitive on-road navigation sensors that would never stand up beyond the controlled environment of CityTech and a few selected paths located elsewhere.

The brain surgeon glanced out the window at the emerging urban landscape. So this is the cradle of the coital matrix and the Triple M, he thought. It was worse than he expected. All of the icing and none of the cake. Immaculately landscaped gardens, but with no context, no reason to approach them, no trace of human activity—no bench, no shop, no windows. And indeed, there was no one there. Barely a person had been visible since they left the medical center.

Marilyn parked the hypercush at the main port of Purple Complex. From there, it was a short walk to the secured apartment. Forrester was reunited with his luggage, brought in earlier that day by his new roommate, Thomas. Thomas was one of the Root's leading weapons and explosives specialists, and, by trade, a gardener and carpenter. He had found a job doing landscape maintenance at Purple Complex. Marilyn introduced the two operatives, and showed Forrester to his room.

Thomas had prepared some tea for the weary duo, who, despite their fatigue, knew that an initial briefing could not be delayed. It was necessary to synchronize a number of behaviors, ranging from frequency and mode of contact to emergency procedures in the event of a "collapse," the discovery of their mission by the authorities. Thomas also described in detail the secured apartment.

After sleeping for twelve hours, Forrester awoke, disoriented in his new surroundings. It took several minutes to clear his mental fog, composed of leftover images from dreams mixed with fears, worry, and some pain in various parts of his body. He pulled himself together and looked at the surroundings, feeling rather gloomy. When he limped his way into the main room, Marilyn was waiting at the dining table. She had taken the day off to help her new colleague get settled in. She greeted Forrester and began to prepare breakfast.

He sighed and slowly took a seat. He dreamily watched Marilyn move to and fro, which she did with a delicate feminine rapidity. Everything about her, the easy bounce of her hair, the way she mumbled instructions to herself, the occasional smile in his direction, caused him to experience a sentiment of airtight trust. Again he thought of her personal story, and the dangers involved in the mission, and had to fight back his tears. O Lord, he implored silently, protect this fine creature.

He studied the interior of the flat. The floor plan was well-designed, but the appointments were as cold and inhuman as the landscaping he had seen the day before. There was no color to speak of, everything being decorated in shades of gray. Flashy metallic surfaces abounded. The lighting, he noticed, was adequate and well-recessed, but it emitted a strange glow.

Breakfast was served and the duo got down to business. Forrester would begin work the next day. He needed to concoct various pretexts for leaving work early in order to have adequate time to execute his real tasks. At the outset, much of his evening time would be spend in front of the flat's computer, collecting every manner of relevant information. He would also find the opportunity to observe Harris's Blue Complex and the various places frequented by him. After a week or two of this field work, a decision would be made as to how contact with Harris should be initiated.

From conversations with Marilyn and a fat dossier that he studied before his departure from Jeptathia, Forrester already had acquired a solid foundation. He knew that Harris had grown up in the same environment and at the same time as Marilyn, and had witnessed the horrors of the Bombardments. Yet he did not turn against the perpetrators of the carnage. Granted, he lost only one relative (a cousin) and two or three acquaintances, but the entire sector of the city in which he spent his childhood was reduced to a pile of rubble. He seems to have been as enthusiastic as anyone about the newly-founded WestTech zone. Forrester learned that Harris turned in a brilliant performance at the Academy, where he pursued advanced study in cyberengineering and biochemistry. His thesis on some of the more theoretical aspects of heliovision was a pioneering work.

It was here that the mystery grew thicker. Why did he end up working at such a mediocre shop as InterFun? And why did he get pigeonholed, always relegated to the company's second or third tier? He spent years on the same treadmill. If he had wanted to go to CityTech or even upgrade his employment at WestTech, what could have stopped him? Instead, Harris let himself sink into near oblivion.

Another strange aspect of the case, thought Forrester, was the heliovision expert's lifestyle. It was a solitary existence, with scant romantic engagements and no close friends. This was combined with the gamut of banal WestTech amusements, most of them drawing heavily on a mix of mood-altering substances and outrageous public spectacles. In and of itself, this was not in the least unusual. In fact, it was typical of the population. What distinguished Harris was his intelligence and professional potential. Clearly, something was awry when a person of such stature, at the early-middle segment of his career, had a lifestyle suited to a dropout. Even in WestTech, conjectured Forrester, the distractions of the elite must be slightly more refined than a constant diet of bunga nuts, dive-bombing, and cerebral plunges.

Another factor was the death or disappearance, in the years just before and since the Division, of nearly all of Harris's close relatives. Of course, one had to factor into the equation the developments in WestTech culture, where many people maintained little or no contact with family. Thus Harris would not necessarily feel in any way deviant. Yet the mourning process, particularly in the early years, must have taken its toll, not to mention the long periods of solitude that followed.

Over the next few days, Forrester settled into his new job. Most of the time he was shuttled back and forth by Marilyn. The office environment was upbeat and friendly. At certain moments, he would forget his mission and react to people normally, as if this were his regular life. Whenever he snapped out of the illusion, he had to endure several minutes of sorrow and emotional pain. Often this triggered a further descent into regret and self-doubt. He worried about the mission. He worried about Marilyn. He worried about the fate of mankind.

One evening, while conducting research on the computer, Forrester was engaged in a bout of self-deprecation. Perhaps he should have swallowed his pride, he thought, and rejected the mission. Wasn't there something he could have done for the cause in Jeptathia? Was it necessary to send a taciturn, limping old man on a mission for which perfect physical condition and nerves of steel were de rigueur? Why did he have to be a hero—wasn't it enough that he sacrificed a glamorous career and spent the last two decades of his life in a slum? And what's the difference, anyway. Could they realistically hope to stop the TransTech world dead in its tracks? What pretension! This fearsome Root couldn't organize its way out of a paper bag. It would be a miracle, thought Forrester, if the whole mission wasn't botched before they even made contact with Harris.

He emerged from his reverie to find himself hunched over and looking straight down at his lap. In his peripheral vision he saw Thomas crossing the room to open the front door. Without moving his spine, he rotated his head slightly to catch a glimpse of Marilyn stepping into the flat. She saw him and jerked to a halt.

"He's been like that for about ten minutes," reported Thomas. "I didn't know whether I should disturb him."

Marilyn pulled up a chair alongside the impromptu patient, looked him in the eye, and burst out laughing. Forrester was taken aback, but after considering his ridiculous posture, joined in the merriment. Thomas did his part as well, and the three agents let loose a prolonged bout of rambunctious laughter.

Forrester ended the levity by leaning back in his chair with a heavy sigh. He shifted his weight to one side, so that his upper torso rested on the roll of fat above his waist. His associate looked on with an air of compassion. Forrester, with knitted brow, asked Marilyn to update him on the current state of cyberbiological development in CityTech.

She spelled out, in great detail, the latest trends. This included Triple M, heliovision, the embracer, the Dome, and Harris's role in all of them. Forrester listened attentively to every word. He chewed on the inside of his cheek until it was sore. By the end of the story, all of his guilt had dissipated. He fathomed the situation, and it was almost too heavy to bear. He closed his eyes as his heart sank to the ground. So, he said to himself, it has come to this. The moment has arrived to jettison all fear, inhibition, and misplaced pity. He would march forth into the line of fire. His jaws were clenched as he picked up his head, breathed in deeply, and looked directly at Marilyn. She responded with a subtle grin that said, "yes, I've been there too; welcome to the fight."

That evening, he called his wife. To preserve mission security, they were obliged to pretend that all was normal, and that Jessica would be joining him very soon. By using a prearranged system of coded topics, he did his best to reassure her that all was well. For example, the success of the mission was conveyed by talking about the quality of the food in CityTech.

The next day, after taking a short mid-afternoon stroll through the indoor office and commercial complex attached to the medical center, Forrester entered the center's lobby through one of the main doors. As he passed through, a man's shoulder hit his own, lightly knocking him sideways. He looked back; their eyes locked as their bodies became momentarily immobilized. It was Harris. Forrester wanted to seize the opportunity, but remained still, mouth agape, for several seconds.

Harris reacted first, raising his hands in a gesture of apology before continuing his hurried trot into the building.

During the hypercush ride back to Purple Complex that evening, Marilyn was noticeably agitated. She decided to violate security regulations by discussing a sensitive subject outside of the secured apartment. "You'll never believe this," she said. "I overheard a conversation in the cafeteria. They were saying that the final treatment of the embracers, for the last six weeks, has been taking place right under our noses, right at our medical center."

"Interesting," said Forrester. "And I literally bumped into our dear Harris coming into the building this morning. Something's up."

They agreed that some immediate investigative work was in order. An hour or so of poking around on the computer and a couple of conversations at the office the next day yielded a number of salient facts. It turned out that indeed, much of the recent treatment of the embracers had been taking place at the medical center. Moreover, a new "class" had arrived only a fortnight before, following several months of preparatory work elsewhere. Now they were beginning the physical transformation itself. There was an entire department consecrated to the effort, and it was shrouded in mystery. The staff was told that it was a special project involving advanced research in sexual dysfunction.

At their evening discussion, Marilyn mentioned that she was friendly with the manager of the lab, Olivia Gardner. The two agents agreed that Marilyn would approach her without delay.

The following day, Marilyn contacted Gardner to invite her to an impromptu coffee break, mentioning that Forrester would be in attendance. Naturally, Gardner was only too pleased to have the chance to chat with the legendary brain surgeon. As they sipped their respective refreshments, Forrester explained his interest in the link between the brain and sexual desire. Gardner's ego was tickled pink when Marilyn proposed, off-handedly, a tour of the more interesting parts of the lab, those related to the research in sexual dysfunction.

"Well," exclaimed the lab manager, looking at Forrester, "you must be involved in the special project."

"Not really," he replied. "I'll probably be joining in a bit later. I was asked to participate, but I've begun so many new projects that I'm really in over my head."

As soon as the glasses were empty, the trio headed for the lab. "Over here we have a variety of skin samples," said Gardner, gesturing toward a collection of glass preservation tanks. Marilyn began a rapid-fire question and answer session, feigning an extreme interest in the most obscure details of laboratory science. This freed up Forrester to sniff around the lab. He began to view the samples in the tanks. They contained skin fragments in a variety of textures and colors, apparently part of an effort to produce a grayish tone.

Forrester glanced back at Gardner, whose mouth was in high gear, egged on by Marilyn's continual look of amazement. He turned his attention toward the far wall. There was an exposition of small body parts, which he discerned to be various glands. Looking further, he stopped dead in his tracks. To an experienced surgeon, there was no mistaking the sight of human testicles, although it took a couple of seconds for the idea to sink in. There were at least a dozen pairs, neatly arranged in a row. Forrester forced himself to move on, so as not to attract attention. He concealed his shock in his overall limp, bending over and coughing a bit more than usual. He would not be able to share the discovery with his loyal compatriot until evening.

That afternoon, Forrester and Marilyn attended a press conference held by BrainHost to announce "one of the greatest developments of all time in the field of cyberbiology." The press room resembled a small theatre, with graduated rows seating about a hundred people. Each seat was equipped with a datapad and a translation device. The walls were splattered with awards and memorabilia, including a photo of Megan Bullock's inauguration ceremony. There were also a couple of pieces of expensive contemporary art.

The CEO herself approached the podium to host the festivities. Harris, along with Amrake, Humboldt-Weizmann, and a couple of board members, sat at the dais. William Nice was absent because of an important meeting involving the embracers. Forrester and Marilyn sat near the back of the theater, in the section reserved for members of the scientific community. Forrester looked on with a mixture of dread and fascination. This Harris fellow, he thought, always looks a bit embarrassed and out of place, though at the same time very serious and absorbed in his task. The same disposition he had exhibited when the two collided at the door of the medical center.

Bullock was as expressionless as a boulder when she began her remarks. She let slip the slightest grin, however, when announcing that "the rumors you've been hearing—well, they're true. Heliovision is a fact, it's happening." She proceeded to explain the rationale for pursuing the project, the R&D timetable (including the release of the alpha version just two weeks hence), and the key role played by Harris. It was to be nothing short of a new era, and, she added parenthetically, there would be plenty of subcontracting and spin-off work to keep the entire TransTech world busy for the next five years. She left the podium to a round of tumultuous applause. Next it was Harris's turn. He laid out, in very broad terms, the more technical aspects of the project.

Forrester cringed. If the remarks he had just heard were to be taken at face value, the project was further along than he had estimated.

When the presentation ended, the audience was invited to partake in a magnificent buffet of biogenerative foodstuffs, including some of the most tender sandlubbers that money could buy. A crowd swarmed around Harris. Marilyn dragged her cohort over as fast as she could, but they were forced to take up position about three layers out. Finally, after ten minutes or so of jockeying, they found themselves just inches from their target. Marilyn blasted her way into the conversation, asking Harris whether he remembered her, and then introduced Forrester as an accomplished expert in neurology who yearned to get involved in heliovision. But no sooner had the two scientists shook hands that Amrake came over and whispered a few words in Harris's ear. The star of the show withdrew from the forum, apologizing profusely to all present that he was being summoned to an urgent meeting.

"Damn," exclaimed Marilyn. "After all that effort." Forrester, though, was positive, saying that the direct contact, however brief, was well worth the entire outing. That was all he needed in order to formally request a meeting, or to find another way to put himself in Harris's presence.

That evening at the secured apartment, Forrester related his discovery at the lab. Marilyn looked disgusted but not shocked. "Everybody knows they're conducting surgery on their volunteers," she said. "The fact that they're being neutered doesn't surprise me in the least."

The next item on the Root operatives' agenda was how to make contact with Harris. Marilyn suggested a stakeout at the Sidewalk Café. Forrester rejected the idea, saying that more strident action was called for. With the alpha release of heliovision just two weeks away, time was running out. He would communicate with Harris forthwith, spelling out his credentials, his research, his desire for a meeting, and the potential benefits for BrainHost. He proceeded to compose the following letter:

Dear Sir,

Permit me to introduce myself. I am a great admirer of your work in the field of heliovision, and in other branches of cyberbiology. My background is in neurology, and I am a practicing brain surgeon. I earned my medical degree and PhD in organic chemistry some 35 years ago at the WestTech Academy (it had a different name then), where I understand you also studied.

I recently arrived in your fascinating locale in my new role as senior research fellow at the CityTech Medical Center. In this capacity, I have begun conducting advanced study on the link between the brain and sexual desire. I have attached a copy of my CV, along with my latest article in the *Journal of Brain Tissue,* to give you an idea of my work.

It would please me greatly to have the opportunity to meet with you. I believe we can help each other. To name but one example, I am in touch with individuals who are conducting research on the alteration, via neurosurgery and chemical manipulation, of sexual images in the mind. This may interest you, being that it is highly relevant to your work.

I look forward to meeting you at your earliest convenience.

Sincerely,

Dr. Ebenezer Forrester

Marilyn read the letter, and gave her approval. She did, however, make one small correction, replacing "Dear Sir" with the current CityTech usage, "To the recipient." Forrester sent the message. Less than half an hour later, a brief response arrived, proposing a meeting at Harris's office the very next day.

The following morning at the medical center passed slowly for Forrester, eager as he was to meet with Harris. As he pretended to read an article on brain cells, his mind wandered to some of the events of recent days. His thoughts were dominated by the glass containers in the lab. It was an unforgettable image.

Finally, the hour arrived. After passing through the security rig at the entrance to BrainHost, a guard escorted Forrester to Harris's door. He limped through the jaws of the furry pig, and was led by Harris to the mini conference area. The two engaged in a round of pleasantries, which was followed by an awkward silence, heavy with anticipation. The brain surgeon then delved into an explanation of his work.

Harris was only half concentrating. He did not recall ever seeing such a face or hearing such a speech pattern. The closest thing were the outerwarts he met when purchasing the synchbox in Jeptathia, but even they did not equal this specimen. And this is a brain surgeon? Harris suppressed a chuckle. Where did they dig this wart up? Maybe he belongs to the group that can perform complex mathematical calculations in their heads. And now he *understands*. And what about that strange woman from the medical center he always has at his side, who wanted me to meet him so badly. She always has that condescending smile on her face. And now he wants to know all about my work. The whole thing is weird, but maybe it's just another outerwart scrambling to get a piece of the action before their whole rotten society falls apart. It happens every day of the week.

Harris began to explain some of the more esoteric aspects of his own work, and it was Forrester's turn to observe. So this is a prime specimen of *homo transtechus*, he thought. What is that hideous outfit he's wearing? Looks like he's wrapped in polyurethane. They've elevated discomfort to an art. And his eyes—constantly moving, never focused, pupils dilated. Just a reaction machine, a human computer, without the deep inner core that sustains the soul of man. And very soon, their reproductive organs will be in a jar, their brains manipulated, worshipping in cults that gather in domes. Forrester had to stop himself to avoid losing altogether the train of conversation.

"So you see, doctor," summarized Harris, "We're on the verge of a revolutionary change in human behavior, one that has the potential to eliminate almost all stress from our lives. It was discovered that most stress occurs because we are constantly chasing something we cannot have. We are saddled with this drive to unite with another human being, to become one unit. But this can never be attained. Each person, even at the decisive moment, even when there is great physical pleasure involved, fights to maintain his or her own independence. The result is an endless cycle of pain, disappointment, and resentment.

"Society's level of development in the area of sexuality is roughly the equivalent of agricultural development, say, ten thousand years ago. Each person had to satisfy all their own needs, locked in a relentless battle with nature. But later, civilization stepped in to help the individual. Food production became regularized and specialized. And today, you simply order what you want. Well, we're doing the same thing for the human sex life. First, the coital matrix regularizes the process, and, in a way, you can order the dish that you want. No stress is involved, once you've mastered the technique of course, which anyone can do.

"The next step, with heliovision and related discoveries, is to eliminate altogether this savage, inhuman burden, this drive to deprive another person of their freedom, and, by extension, their ability to self-realize. You see, doctor, we now have the means to channel this immense reservoir of energy to other parts of the individual's own body, so that the sexual process is turned around—instead of the deprivation of another's independence, the individual is transformed into a powerhouse of self-realization and freedom. With total spiritual fulfillment and the most intense physical pleasure imaginable thrown into the bargain."

Forrester summoned all of his emotional stamina to maintain his positive facial expression. When Harris finished speaking, leaning back triumphantly in his plush armchair, Forrester tossed a few flattering remarks into the conversation. He restrained his impulse to demolish Harris's reasoning, deferring that pleasure to a more fortuitous venue.

Nevertheless, he deemed it prudent to launch a single probe, for the purpose of testing the cyberengineer's true creed.

"At the medical center, apparently, there's some work going on in the very field you just described," said Forrester. He waited for a reaction to his salvo, but Harris was impassible, allowing just a look of mild curiosity. "I don't know much about it," he continued. "By coincidence, I was in the lab the other day for something else, and I saw a few shelves dedicated to some tests going on. It looks like they're trying to attain a certain skin tone. I think they've gone a bit heavy on the melanin. And those glands," added Forrester, nonchalantly and with a warm smile, "I have to say, I did feel a little uncomfortable seeing someone's gonads in a jar, if you know what I mean."

Harris maintained his frozen expression, but this time he turned pale. "Are you sure that's what it was?"

"There's no mistaking it."

"Maybe it's part of some other research or treatment. The lab down there must have body parts galore."

"Maybe you're right," admitted Forrester.

"You mentioned in your letter that you know some people working on the alteration of sexual images in the mind."

"Yes, that's right."

"Are they interested in a deal?"

"Probably. It doesn't do them any good to keep it to themselves."

"Please look into it for me."

"I will."

After Forrester departed, Harris signaled Mr. J., who was observing the interview from the next room via hidden camera. The security chief came in and joined him in the conference area. "You were absolutely right to alert us," he said. "We just checked out his apartment, it's been secured, wired to the hilt. It's time to bring him in."

Harris nodded, but felt remorse at his betrayal of Forrester. The man was a spy for the Root, Harris reminded himself, there was no longer any question. Yet he was also one of the most accomplished researchers of his generation, personally responsible for some of the most impressive medical advancements in recent years. What a waste, thought Harris; what a pity.

He looked at Mr. J. "Is there a way to save him? I mean, not for his sake, but for ours? He would be extremely valuable to our work on heliovision and other projects."

"Yes, I know what you mean," said Mr. J., without emotion. "Well, he didn't kill anyone, but of course we don't know what they were hatching over there. Look, if you can get him to cooperate with us, lead us to other Root operatives, and then submit to one of our retraining programs, maybe we can make a deal."

"Excellent," said Harris.

"Hang on, though," said Mr. J., raising his hand as if to stop traffic. "If it turns out he was planning to kill someone or destroy some building, there's nothing I can do. It would be out of my hands immediately. But assuming that's not the case, I think we can hold him for a few days. I'll have to clear it with Davis over at Justice, but he owes me one."

"Thanks," said Harris, shaking the security chief's hand.

"Don't get your hopes up. I think he's a diehard. You can talk to him, though. I'll be watching from the side. If he takes your bait, and it looks clean to me, I'll plead your case to the Justice people. Anyway, I know that it would be great for the company if it worked out."

Harris didn't hear the last sentence. He was already pondering the appeal he would make to Forrester.

CHAPTER SEVEN

▼

An hour later, Forrester was being held in a secret, high-security detention center not far from the Nice estate. Mr. J. and several officers took him into custody as he was about to enter the medical center. The center was notified that Forrester had fallen ill, and would be resting for a few days at the home of a friend. Meanwhile, the special forces unit of the CityTech police stormed the secured apartment. Thomas was killed trying to escape, but not before he notified the people in Jeptathia of what was transpiring.

Fortunately for Marilyn, Forrester had an inkling that something was awry in the meeting with Harris. His suspicion was confirmed when Harris agreed too quickly and too smoothly to pursue a deal with Forrester's unnamed associates. Just after leaving the meeting, he contacted Marilyn on his datapad and conveyed the code for mission collapse. She began the pre-established procedure to flee CityTech immediately. In her desk, she kept a special bag that was packed and ready for such a contingency. In addition to basic travel items, it contained the forged printout of a message from Jeptathia General Hospital notifying her that her mother was on her deathbed, having only several hours to live.

Marilyn rushed to the roof of the CityTech Medical Center, where, in tears and hospital message in hand, she pleaded for the helicopter ambulance service to ferry her to the airport. On the way, the helicopter pilot arranged for a seat on a cargo flight to Jeptathia. The pilot of the plane, in turn, seeing the young woman in hysterics over her mother, contacted the hospital in Jeptathia, where Root operatives were waiting for the call. They arranged for a car to meet the jet, in order to bring Marilyn directly to her mother. The escape went smoothly, thanks to the extreme rapidity of the departure. She managed to stay one step ahead of the authorities, but barely.

Meanwhile, at the detention center, Harris began to interrogate Forrester in accordance with his loose agreement with Mr. J. The two antagonists eyeballed each other across a simple, wide table. The room was sparse, with a very high ceiling, almost two stories high. Near the top was a mirrored gallery, from where Mr. J. and a security officer observed the proceedings. There was no color to speak of. The ceiling was chock full of lights and audio equipment, which enabled the interrogators to fill the room with almost any imaginable sound and light combination. For the time being, they used a simple, mind-numbing white light, similar to the type that illuminated the corridors of BrainHost.

Forrester braced himself. He surmised that Harris was being used as part of a soft interrogation strategy, perhaps a good cop/bad cop routine. He had no intention of divulging even the slightest detail. Harris looked at the prisoner with his most impassible facial expression. Forrester matched the look with equal fervor. A standoff ensued.

Harris was the first to lose his patience. "Dr. Forrester, let me get to the point. You and I both know that the police are waiting to get their hands on you. But I asked them for some time, in order to pursue my own agenda. In spite of this somber situation, I think there's something we can do that is in our mutual interest. Otherwise..."

"A piece of my anatomy will be floating in formaldehyde."

Harris involuntarily recoiled an inch or two. But he recovered his composure and continued as if nothing had been said. "I would like you to be my research partner."

Forrester displayed a look of surprise. "I guess I should spy more often," he said.

"It may sound odd," admitted Harris. "But with your knowledge of the brain and nervous system, our projects could advance rapidly on several fronts. It would be a tragedy for your expertise to be lost to humanity. Naturally, you have to be willing to turn over a new leaf, to begin a new life. We have people who can help with that. You will see, Dr. Forrester, that in the final analysis we are undertaking the most ambitious attempt ever at human perfection. We have no desire to kill, torture, or cause even the slightest pain to you or anyone else. That's why it was decided that no punishment would be considered before exhausting every possible route of dialogue and reconciliation.

"If you agree to help us with some technical details, and then undergo a special regime of reorientation and relaxation, I might be able to quietly make a deal with the authorities. Keep in mind that your case has not yet been made public." Harris leaned forward onto the table, looking intensely at Forrester. "I want you to join us."

"You would have to give me a lobotomy."

Harris grimaced and cocked his head in a display of impatience. "For your information," he retorted, the volume of his voice escalating, "what you saw in the lab is part of a very important process. The individuals involved are doing this on a volunteer basis—we don't force anyone to do anything in CityTech—and they have already reaped huge personal reward, not to mention the contribution they've made to the happiness of future generations." Harris's voice was shaking as he added: "Happiness that will not be wiped out by bombs from the Root or anyone else."

Forrester was observing Harris as the latter let his beliefs be known. So this is a leading exponent of "the most ambitious attempt ever at human perfection," he thought. Absolutely brilliant: they're creating a generation of eunuchs who fantasize themselves into a frenzy. What a banal destination for mankind. And how would they procreate, if every person were to become an embracer? Perhaps CloneFarm has another project to solve that problem. Of course, the outerwarts could be a source of raw material.

He resolved to probe Harris's mind. "Tell me something," he said, calmly and soothingly. "As a scientist, what precisely is your objection to the natural, God-given manner of reproduction?"

Harris's ego was awakened by this appeal to his professional opinion. "First of all, as a scientist, I view reality as it is, empirically, with no set of *a priori* assumptions. Therefore, the term God-given has no relevance for me. Second, if we were all bound by natural processes, we would still be living in caves. All of civilization is nothing more than one long struggle to overcome natural processes, to bestow upon the human race more and more freedom, the freedom to shape our world in the most beneficial way possible."

Forrester wondered whether these words were original, or something Nice was preaching at the Dome. He countered: "Yes, I suppose that in my own work I've battled numerous natural processes. But surely you would admit that even when fighting against them, we usually bend and adapt, channeling the forces we find in a productive manner. We thin out the herd, reroute the river, fertilize the soil. In each case, nature is harnessed and put to better use, but not negated. In medicine, we amputate only in the most extreme cases."

Harris waited patiently before responding. "I agree completely. Although it may not seem that way right now, that's exactly what we're doing here. We're using the existing reproductive system as a jumping-off point. Look," he said emphatically, pressing his fingertips together, "the sexual act as we have known it is the last activity to be civilized, to be humanized. In its natural form, it's the equivalent of you and I getting on our hands and knees, sticking our heads in a trough, and chomping on our food like a horse. But of course we don't do that. We sit at a table with plates and silverware. It's the same idea with the coital matrix. The act of intercourse is still performed, just as the food is still eaten at the table. But it has been rerouted, to use your term."

Harris forged ahead, encouraged by Forrester's feigned look of interest. "Sex has been made simple and accessible for millions of individuals who previously experienced it as a minefield. They were forced to pursue relations fraught with deception, domination, abuse; a litany of social ills in their most concentrated form. The result: agony, frustration, hatred, broken lives, loneliness. Not to mention the special problems of women, reduced to the level of beasts of burden, brutalized even in the best of cases. All the sensitivity training in the world couldn't fix that. No, the act itself had to be altered. Using the coital matrix, the woman becomes a full partner—no fear, no domination. And the man, too, is liberated from the onerous pressure to subdue the woman. In short, everyone can now concentrate on one thing, their pleasure. What could be better than that?"

The question was fielded by Forrester's face, but his mind was busy analyzing Harris's features. He noticed that the heliovision expert possessed only a handful of facial expressions, corresponding to several emotional states. Never was a rogue eyebrow raised, nor was there any idiosyncratic curvature of the mouth, and no depth in the eyes. It was as if the head were simply an elaborate calculator, accompanied by several dials indicating its current status, such as temperature or percent of capacity used. In these circumstances, any attempt at argument was futile. Could such a person, reasoned Forrester, have any grasp of love, intimacy, passion? Of truths self-evident across all of time, down to the Division? Perhaps others in CityTech were not beyond the pale, but Harris and his Dome cohorts had crossed the point of no return, at least no return by means of mere discussion.

Forrester realized that Harris was leaning toward him, waiting for an answer. "Yes, yes, that's quite interesting. So far you're rerouting nature. But what about the embracers? That's a different kettle of fish."

Harris pressed his fingertips together with new vigor. "This is something, Dr. Forrester, that you, as a surgeon and medical researcher, can appreciate. It's all about choice. That is, choosing one's path in life, choosing to be liberated. You, doctor, liberate people from disease. We also liberate them from a disease of sorts, or, more accurately, from a burden that stands in the way of their spiritual growth. We're rerouting in the extreme: transforming an oppressive yoke into a tool for the ultimate liberation of humanity. In one fell swoop, the artful combination of heliovision, surgery, and the Dome are united to burst asunder all the chains. It is something that the ancient Greeks must have projected in their wildest fantasies."

Forrester concealed a shiver of disgust. He braced himself for the philosophical underpinnings of the cult of the Dome.

"What is it, doctor, that philosophers, gurus, and other spiritually-inclined individuals have been pursuing since day one? A perfect intellectual state, a perfect peace, a harmony that is undisturbed by any external force. The problem is, what to do with the body. There are two alternatives: neutralize it, or harness it. We have chosen the latter. Instead of being a source of friction, the sexual act will now serve the individual, existing solely for the individual's benefit. Instead of the tragic split between the sexes—an inherently divisive and eternal source of strife—the individual can channel all sides of this explosive impulse to an exclusively personal benefit, and precisely in the manner that most appeals to that individual. By contrast, when there is a clash of desires and egos, the drives are frittered away on senseless warfare. What's more, people waste half their lives trying to make themselves sexually attractive. We believe, doctor, that world peace begins within each and every one of us. You are in favor of peace, Dr. Forrester, aren't you?"

The surgeon could no longer contain himself. "What about love?" he shouted, his face distended from the sudden release of repressed emotion. "Doesn't that mean anything to you?"

Harris seized the opportunity provided by the outburst to grab the moral high ground. With perfect calm, he responded. "Like peace, love begins within us. We must love ourselves in order to be capable of including others in a zone of love that radiates outward from the heart. If that heart is not whole and not satisfied within itself, then it will revert to deception, abuse, and all the other ills. It will exploit others to serve itself, to satisfy its unattained craving. But when two harmonious and satisfied hearts meet, the encounter begins on an equal footing, to everyone's benefit. The motivation for exploitation has been eliminated. This is what happens when two embracers meet. So to answer your question, doctor, we seek to attain a higher, perfected form of love."

A knot of tension had formed in Forrester's gut. He was eating himself alive. This conversation was similar to one he had experienced numerous times in a recurring nightmare. He had felt deep within his soul that one day, it would really take place. There was nowhere to go, nowhere to hide, and no arguments to be made. As he observed Harris, the brain surgeon thought to himself: What could possibly move this man to reconsider his beliefs? He has been extracted from the world, from civilization. He has no god, no love, no wife, no children, no law, no binding ethical code, no roots, no history, no art, no culture. He is alienated from all that has sustained mankind throughout the generations. There is no argument to be made because there is no point of attack nor common ground. The only possibility, and a slim one at that, would be to tempt him with a more enticing form of pleasure.

Harris did not relent. "Another fascinating thing, doctor, is the history of attempts to achieve this perfect love. Of course, over the last century there have been numerous efforts at liberation, at empowering the individual to reach for the forms of self-fulfillment that are uniquely suited to each person. But these efforts were primitive, unassisted by the tools we are developing today. I should add that there is historical precedent for these tools. For example, group rituals, such as the pioneering sexual rites of the Canaanite tribes. Also, certain narcotics have long been used to stimulate personal fulfillment. But all of this is child's play compared to what we're doing today.

"The Dome prepares the individual to become an embracer, or at the very least, to think like one. It's really about casting off the obstacles to our complete self-realization. And what, precisely, does the word heliovision mean? Literally, sun-vision or, alternatively, seeing by means of the sun. The sun is a giant furnace, a meltdown of all elements within it. Everything combined into one mass, operating at maximum power. No contradictions, no divisions, no competing egos. Moreover, it is the ultimate source of all life in our solar system."

Harris halted his speech and contemplated his adversary. None of his words seemed to be penetrating the brain surgeon's defenses. Harris felt a mixture of pity and revulsion. Here was a scientist with a most unscientific mind. How was it possible? Forrester's accomplishments were indisputable, yet he possessed an irrational mind and primitive personality traits. Was he some sort of idiot savant? What other explanation could there be? And getting mixed up with the Root, to top it off. All this talk aimed at making him understand is a waste of time, argued Harris's pessimistic side. You could prove to him that tomorrow he would wake up in a utopia, and he would still carry on about "rerouting" nature.

"Well, doctor, what's your decision?" asked Harris, dryly and mechanically.

"Put me out of my misery," replied Forrester. "I don't want to witness the neutering of mankind."

Harris displayed no emotion. "You still have a few days to reconsider, according to my agreement with the police. After that, you belong to them." He stood up, motioned to the gallery, and headed for the door. A guard escorted Forrester back to his cell.

At that same moment, Marilyn was arriving at the Root facility, the underground hideout, near Jeptathia. Ingerman and several of his top people were waiting for her there. She was informed that Thomas was dead and Forrester was captured. Ingerman, snorting more than usual, sat next to Marilyn to let her know that Forrester would almost certainly be put to death. There was no apparent possibility of escape or rescue, and no reason for the cyberwarts to keep him alive beyond the short time needed to extract all the information that he possessed. Meanwhile, all Root operations were being scrambled and rearranged, so that within less than twenty-four hours, all codes, schedules, aliases, and facilities will have been reshuffled, as if an entirely new organization had been created. This was the third time in Root history that this standard operating procedure had been followed.

Marilyn pressed her hands against the side of her head and let out a wail of anguish. The group watched her moan and cry for some time. As she slumped in her chair and settled into a muffled sobbing, Ingerman began to bark orders to his entourage, and they scattered to their respective tasks. When he was alone with Marilyn, he introduced a ray of hope. "We decided not to inform Forrester's wife because there's still the slightest chance that something can be done."

Marilyn wiped her face and stared at the commander like a child being told that Santa Claus was about to arrive.

"You know about this guy Beecely, Harris's former colleague, right?"

"Yes."

"He hates Harris with a passion, and would probably do just about anything for revenge. In reality, the equations that Harris stole would probably not have made that much of a difference. CityTech would still have the upper hand over WestTech, when it comes to the Triple M. But to the folks at InterFun, Harris wrecked their greatest hope in years."

"So?" asked Marilyn, impatiently.

"Well listen to this. Just to give you an idea of how far Beecely is prepared to go, he contacted us a few days ago, using the same channels he had used to get the synchbox from Thaddeus Jones. He hinted as clearly as he could that he had some dirt on Harris. That's all I know. We stalled for time because I wanted you to be in on this. I'm going to see him in a couple of hours at his hotel room in the TransTech enclave downtown, and you're coming with me."

"Yes!"

"But don't get your hopes up," cautioned the chief. "We both know that the chances of getting Forrester out of there are extremely slim."

The psychologist leaned back in her chair, awash in emotion. She had developed a special affection for Forrester. He was one of the few people she had ever been able to trust with no reservations.

Ingerman contacted an employee of the hotel—a Root agent—and told him to conduct a survey of the area and verify that Beecely's room and its immediate vicinity were secure. The Root commander and Marilyn followed close behind. They met Beecely in a small, simple room. He was alone. Ingerman introduced himself and Marilyn using phony names, and claiming that they were associates of Thaddeus Jones.

"So," said the chief, "how can we help each other?"

Beecely's back and neck stiffened as his lips pressed together. "You know as well as I do what this guy Harris did to us. We have some information about him that, if made known to the CityTech public, would sink his ship. You have connections over there. You could help with the publicity." Beecely lowered his voice: "And there's money in it for you."

Marilyn had the urge to jump up in a fit of joy, but held fast.

"Can you tell us something about this information?" ventured Ingerman, maintaining perfect calm.

"Harris could have had a brilliant career, but he was plagued by a singular flaw in his personality—kleptomania. There was apparently no limit to what he would steal, forge, and sell in order to advance himself. Of course, in the end, it was counterproductive." Beecely paused, shaking his head. "I was teaching at the Academy in those days," he continued, in a nostalgic tone. "Harris was a near-genius, top of his class. I covered up for him several times. After the last of these incidents, the administration was on the verge of throwing him out, stripping him of all diplomas and citations. I managed to put out the fire and quietly slide him into an obscure mid-level job at InterFun, where I myself had just accepted the post of head of R&D." Beecely opened his palms upward in a gesture of frustration. "I saved his neck, and look where it got me."

He divulged several details concerning Harris's alleged misconduct, leaving no doubt as to the scandalous nature of the charges, and claimed that he could back everything up with indisputable documentation. Ingerman asked for a two-hour break, during which time he would consult with his colleagues and return with a response to Beecely's proposal.

Twenty minutes later, Marilyn and Ingerman were in conference with Reginald Burns, one of Ingerman's closest associates. He was known to Marilyn, who participated with him in some explosives training about nine months earlier. The present meeting took place in the basement of a new safe house deep within the slums of Jeptathia, hastily set up in accordance with the Root shakeup. Ingerman reviewed the big picture: Operations in CityTech would now be severely hampered, if not suspended, by the collapse of the previous mission. Extreme caution was necessary. The question was, could they still operate in CityTech freely enough to get to Harris and credibly threaten him with dissemination of Beecely's damning information?

Marilyn's face adopted a look of gravity. "There's no one left in CityTech. The only remote possibility is Robertson, but he has no connections. And of course he's keeping a low profile right now." She paused, her eyebrows crunched together. "I'll do it."

"What?" exclaimed the chief. "No way. We send people on dangerous missions, but we're not yet into suicides, especially when there's no possible benefit. They'll nail you the second you show up in CityTech."

"Not if we arrange safe passage in advance, or better yet, force Harris to come over here, to us," responded Marilyn, glowing with pride from her bold idea. "What I'm saying is, present him with an ultimatum: Bring us Forrester or else."

"Forget about it," said Burns. "Beecely has some good dirt, but not that good. Harris is too shrewd to risk his neck just because he might be embarrassed by something that happened years ago. No, we need something fresh, something that would blow him out of the water."

A silence followed. Marilyn pressed her brain to full throttle, turning the situation over and over in her mind. She told her associates about the scene in the laboratory with Olivia Gardner, and what Forrester had witnessed. Perhaps that could be developed into some kind of scandal, she suggested. The other two rejected the idea. Again, it had potential, but there needed to be something altogether damning.

Burns lifted up his head, looking vaguely at the ceiling in the manner of someone developing an idea. "Maybe we need to chat up Beecely. This guy has connections all over the place, he knows the players, he hates Harris and BrainHost, and he knows the technology. What's his story, anyway? Can he be trusted? Is all this just a personal vendetta, or is there some latent sympathy for our cause?" The last question was aimed at Ingerman.

"Beecely has been a mystery right from the start," responded the chief. "There's no reason to believe that he's with us, but then again, no reason to believe that he's not."

Burns turned toward Marilyn. "Why didn't you do this research before, when you could operate freely over there?" he blurted. "Why are all our missions botched like this?" He crossed his arms and legs and leaned away from the other two.

"Take it easy," retorted Ingerman. "If I had five more agents like Marilyn, I'd be governor of CityTech."

Burns calmed himself. "All right, all right," he said, throwing his hands up in frustration. "Go back to Beecely and see what you can get. Now if you'll excuse me, I have to take care of some other business." He left the room.

Marilyn and Ingerman resolved to go back to Beecely with a demand for more information. They would gently broach the subject of the embracers, and see whether Beecely grabbed the bait.

He did. After they returned to the hotel room, Ingerman briefly explained why they considered the "kleptomania approach" to be insufficiently scandalous. He then alluded to the embracers. Beecely lowered his head, looking away in shame. After a long silence, he spoke up.

"Yes, I know all about that. I took part in much of the early research at CloneFarm, and then stayed involved until fairly recently. But things got out of hand. There was the part you alluded to, and other problems, which I won't go into right now." He looked up with a pained expression on his face and beads of sweat on his forehead. "If you don't mind, I'd like to speak to the young lady alone."

Ingerman immediately stood up. "I'll wait in the lobby," he announced, and exited the room.

Beecely continued, his voice shaking. "For some reason, I think I can trust you. Your buddy over there gives me the creeps." He related that the last batch of embracers ran into severe difficulties at CloneFarm, thus for the past three months, work had taken place exclusively in CityTech. This was designed to let the CloneFarm problems blow over. Again, no details were offered. Beecely insisted that his name never be connected with the affair. In fact, this would likely be the last time he ever spoke to her or any of her associates.

The continuation was simple: Within several hours he would send Marilyn the address of the sole survivor of the last batch of embracers. She could then do as she pleased—but never mention Beecely to anyone. "Don't worry," he added, "You'll get your juicy scandal, more than you bargained for." They stood up, and moved toward the door. "Good luck," said Beecely. "It may not seem like it, but I admire your courage. You just jump in there and risk your life, something I was afraid to do."

Marilyn and the chief returned to the safe house. They were joined there by several other Root agents. Marilyn, exhausted, turned on the computer and awaited the promised communiqué from Beecely. She reclined on the adjacent couch, and soon fell into a deep sleep. Two hours later, she was woken up by Ingerman tapping her shoulder. "The computer wants you," he announced. She forced herself out of the slumber, sat up, and extended her arms toward the machine.

Beecely had delivered. The anonymous message, sent from a public computer, was simple and unambiguous: Go alone, immediately, to an address in the mountainous eastern fringe of WestTech, some 350 miles from Jeptathia. Travel under a false identity as a cyberwart from WestTech looking for a spot at which to relax for several days. The destination was an old farm converted into a resort offering short-term cabin rentals. The people she needed to see were there. Once she saw them, the next step would be obvious.

Chapter Eight

▼

Marilyn departed within the hour, with a false passport and driver's license issued in the name of Melinda Pryce, resident of the Coast. She was given a quick makeover, becoming a redhead with closely cropped hair. The Root skin specialist was on hand to give her freckles, a tan, a scar on her neck, and fake fingerprints. She donned a variety of jewelry. The new Melinda, a psychologist returning to WestTech after conducting behavioral research among the outerwarts, was taken by car to an obscure border crossing next to the WestTech village of Frendo, in the foothills some two hundred miles northwest of Jeptathia. The supervisor of the Frendo border station, a Root agent, slipped her through. Once on the WestTech side, she contacted another agent, who had prepared a car with license plates and registration in her assumed name.

Marilyn drove rapidly on the freeway. In rural areas of the TransTech world, the old pre-Division automobile highway system was still very much in use. The terrain turned from semi-arid hills to pine forest to rocky slope as altitude increased, first to seven thousand feet for a bit, and then to nine thousand. The breathtaking scenery could not alleviate the anxiety, impatience, and anger that circulated in her head like an agitated tiger in a cage. She concluded that there was no choice: she must succeed. Forrester's life was hanging in the balance, not to mention the success of the entire anti-heliovision effort. Marilyn cut her lip from the constant biting. At one point, she pulled off the road and cried uncontrollably for several minutes. She then resumed her journey with relative calm, forcing upon herself a cold, steely resolve.

She exited the freeway onto a secondary highway, which soon began to wind its way down into a deep, wide valley. Known for its abundant streams, forests, and wildlife, the valley was a popular tourist spot. After some time, she reached her destination. An old wooden sign announced the "R&R Retreat: Vacation Rentals." She turned and followed the winding private road for about a mile and a half through the woods, up to a clearing that contained a large farmhouse, a parking lot, a red barn, and several small shack-like structures.

Marilyn parked the car and stepped out. The late-morning air was crisp and thin. Some birds could be heard chirping in the distance. The natural surroundings, however, were far from the Root agent's consciousness. She entered the main building. Without any complications, she rented a cabin for one week. The clerk informed her that lunch would be served one hour later in the dining hall at the back of the building.

The cabin was located about a hundred yards away. Marilyn walked there, rolling her suitcase behind her. In her cabin, she showered and changed clothes, stepping into the role of the stressed cyberwart on vacation. She stretched out on the bed and began a controlled-breathing exercise. This quasi-meditation, in the manner of an actor preparing for a performance, was designed to help agents relax, clear their minds, and concentrate fully on the task at hand. Marilyn used the exercise to complete her transformation into Melinda Pryce, a personage modeled after some of her cyberwart acquaintances in CityTech: nervous, assertive, self-absorbed, and above all, thirsting for the latest social conventions. Upon completing the exercise, she stood up, looked at herself in the full-length mirror, fought back a sob from the depth of her chest cavity, and stiffened her back. Her arms were stretched downward, ending in tightly clenched fists. The psychologist-cum-cyberwart was ready for battle.

Melinda Pryce entered the dining room a bit early, in order to have her pick of seating locations. She sat along the wall near the entrance, giving her a full view of the unfolding drama. Little by little the other guests filed in. The group was characterized by older, somewhat moneyed WestTechers. Nearby conversations turned on investments, great vacation spots, the poor service at the R&R Retreat, and the competitive situation of WestTech vis-à-vis the rest of the TransTech world. Melinda quietly munched her filet of dectopus (a recently-developed aquatic creature) and absorbed the new environment.

And then it arrived. A human form, wrapped in a heavy woolen garment, was being pushed in a wheelchair by a huge, abundantly muscled young man. They came to a stop at a small nearby table that had only one chair. Marilyn could not help but gape, as did several other patrons. The human was extremely thin, covered from head to toe except for the face, and slumped deep within the disproportionately large wheelchair. Its skin had a ghastly blend of brown and silver tones. Its face was shriveled and rodent-like, resembling a bat. Marilyn was reminded of a shrunken head she had once seen in a museum. There was no mistaking it: this was the embracer of whom Beecely had spoken, the sole survivor of the ill-fated batch.

That afternoon, Marilyn went down to the small beach along the lake. She opened a deck chair and stretched out. A number of people were swimming in the fresh, clear water. A middle-aged couple entered the scene, unfolding their chairs not two yards from Marilyn. They had an unmistakable air of nouveau riche about them: The man was wearing snapsuit swimming trunks of the Le Blagueur brand, with the telltale zigzag across the crotch. The woman was carrying an "exosac" made from dectopus tentacles. The exosac was covered in tiny suction cups, to which one attached one's keys, wallet, and other accessories. Marilyn held back a chuckle as she viewed this caricature of chic dysfunction.

No sooner had they installed themselves than the couple begin looking around for admiration. Marilyn took the bait. "Wow, is that an exosac?" she asked, in her finest schoolgirl naïveté.

The face of the suction-cup owner announced its satisfaction even before the voice responded. "Yes, I just picked it up last week on sale at La Boutique."

"Oh, I love that place," replied Melinda Pryce, "all kinds of wartish things."

A lively conversation ensued. Melinda revealed that she worked for FolieFrame, a company making software for psychologists, and that she was so stressed out lately that even a cerebral plunge was of little use—thus her escape to the R&R Retreat. The couple were named

Craig Bataglia-Hupert and Jennifer Elliot-Coopers. They resided in a villa ("just a little one") on the Coast, and managed assets for a living.

Marilyn waited for a lull in the conversation to begin her information mining. "Hey, did you two see that poor thing in the wheelchair? What on earth happened?"

Bataglia-Hupert's face turned somber. "Yes, we're already used to it. He—or is it she, I don't know—lives here permanently, it seems. Rumor has it that it's some type of rare cancer."

"I spoke to him once for a few minutes," added Elliot-Coopers. "A real manic-depressive if I ever saw one. And paranoid too."

"That's terrible," said Marilyn. "Maybe I can help him. I'm a psychologist by profession, and I used to specialize in post-traumatic stress disorder."

The couple returned to their cabin for a pre-supper nap. Marilyn remained on the beach, which by now was deserted. After a few minutes had passed, she considered going back to her cabin, since there was not much to be gained by remaining there alone. But then, out of the corner of her eye, she perceived some movement. As the forms moved closer, she turned her head: it was the embracer and its bodyguard. She tried to appear nonchalant as the wheelchair and its occupant came to a stop not far from where the exosac had been.

For almost twenty minutes they sat side-by-side without acknowledging each other's presence. Marilyn decided that she could not delay an initiative any longer. She looked, almost stared, at the eyes of the embracer. It was the reflection of a soul that had been stripped of its dignity, humiliated in the extreme. Marilyn was stunned, not able to find words with which to express herself. She presented a shocked, deeply sympathetic face. The embracer dispatched a furtive glance in her direction. Apparently, it appreciated the honest warmth. Its look of fear diminished somewhat, making way for the slightest smile.

Marilyn regained her composure, sat up straight, pulled back her hair from the side of her face, and addressed this most singular being. "Is this your usual vacation spot?" she ventured.

"Well, I sort of live here, that is, temporarily," replied the embracer, in a screechy, high-pitched voice that matched its rodent-like appearance.

"Oh, I see," said Marilyn. "Yes, it's nice here. Very relaxing."

"And what about you?" asked the embracer, thrilled to find such a nice person with whom to converse.

"I'm here just for a week or so. Getting away from the old computer for a while. By the way, my name is Melinda. I'm a psychologist, now in software, but I used to specialize in post-traumatic stress disorder." She wanted to retract the words the moment they left her mouth.

The embracer was taken aback, scrunching its face at the very hint of something connected to its condition.

"Oh, but that's not important right now. We can't always be working, right? Tell me, what does one do around here for fun?" The last question was posed with such good cheer and such a sincere smile that the embracer was lulled back into its previous state of complicity.

"I don't know," it said, in a soft voice, "but I like to sit by the lake in the evening. That might not be fun, but it's quiet and relaxing."

"Yeah, that's the kind of fun I was thinking about," said Melinda.

"Maybe I'll see you again sometime down here. I have to go now, I can't stay outside too long." The embracer motioned to the guard, and they soon disappeared from the scene. So ended Marilyn's first contact with the person who held the keys to her salvation.

She returned to the lake after supper, but there was no sign of the embracer. After waiting for an hour, she went back to her cabin. She tried desperately to relax, using some of the techniques she had learned in Root training. There was some improvement, but still a knot of frustration and anxiety remained. She eyed her suitcase, which contained an emergency cerebral plunge, but the circumstances did not yet warrant such measures, and besides, she needed all her wits about her. She made one more trip to the lake, with the same result.

The next day, at breakfast and lunch, there was still no sign of the embracer. Marilyn's nerves were becoming frayed. What if it departed? What if it became suspicious—or maybe the guard had some role in all of this. Had the mission collapsed, with her about to be eliminated? Perhaps they had been onto her from the moment she crossed the Line. She began to feel ill. At mid afternoon, she returned to her cabin, politely refusing an invitation from the exosac lady to do some canoeing on the lake.

After supper, Marilyn sat on a bench not far from the main building. A large, dark van pulled into the parking lot. Her heart was pounding.

One of the rear side doors slid open, and out came the embracer and its guard. The driver exchanged a few words with the guard before leaving. The duo headed for their cabin. Marilyn was swept by a wave of relief. But why did they leave? A hundred explanations passed through her mind.

Later that evening, she again headed for the lake. The embracer was already there, more wrapped than usual. The guard was relaxing on a deck chair about eight or ten yards away. Marilyn approached slowly, within the embracer's line of sight, so as not to startle it. At about five paces away, she stopped, cocked her head to one side, waved her hand back and forth, and said hi.

The embracer reacted with a definitive smile, and returned the greeting.

"Can I join you?" she asked. Approval was immediately forthcoming. She pulled over a chair, spying the guard out of the corner of her eye. He seemed aware of all that was taking place, without looking directly at her. "By the way," she said, after settling into her chair, "what's your name?"

The embracer tightly shut its eyes. "I don't have one anymore."

"What do you mean?" asked the psychologist, knowing the possible reason, but still with a bit of incredulity.

"That's a long story," it sighed. "Once I was named Paul. Then I made some changes in my life, and was supposed to be called Unity. But those changes didn't work out." It looked away with tears in its suffocated eyes. "You probably don't want to hear my pathetic story."

Marilyn concealed an explosion of joy, and reverted to being the attentive therapist. "Sure I do—that is, if you want to tell me," she said, in the most soothing of tones.

Unity hesitated for a moment, and then, feigning a bout of chest pain, sent the guard to the cabin to fetch some medicine. It launched into its savage tale. Some five years previously, Paul Bradley-Conrad was a successful 37 year-old real estate broker on the Coast. After his third divorce, he began a tailspin into drugs, outrageous sexual adventures, and cults of every imaginable variety. After nearly two years of this lifestyle, there was nowhere left to go. No brain-fulfillment ritual, public spectacle, or sexual variation could still excite him. He embarked on a desperate effort to find the ultimate stimulation. This effort, pursued with total abandon, led him into contact with people in the cyberbiological world who told him about the work going on at CloneFarm.

After a preliminary screening, Paul Bradley-Conrad was informed that volunteers were needed for "the boldest attempt in history to attain a state of perfect happiness." It involved, ultimately, the ability to physically and emotionally experience—entirely within one's own body—any sexual fantasy one could imagine. "I had to sign a pile of disclaimers, but I didn't care. All I wanted was this super, unprecedented high. I was blinded by my cravings and by my ego."

Marilyn was moved by what she heard, even though she already knew the broad outlines of the story. To hear it told by a survivor was altogether different.

The embracer went on. The group of volunteers was evenly split between men and women, with a number of other attributes controlled to match their proportion within the general population: income, race (in five broad categories), and educational background, among others. It was to be a microcosm of humanity, as befits the inauguration of a new era. The group was cut off from the outside world, sent to a retreat where the climate was ideal. They were subjected to a rigorous regime of physical exercise, strictly controlled diet, and meditation. Next came the drugs: some of the substances were designed to alter the body's normal rhythm, such as the balance of hormones, whereas others were sophisticated narcotics. Yet another stage was neurosurgery, to enable auto-hallucination and to manipulate the link between perception and sexual arousal.

Unity sighed. "Up to that point, everything was great. I was flying high; able to, well, achieve sexual fulfillment in ways you couldn't imagine." But then, it explained, the complications began, in the wake of surgery on the sexual organs. Its organs were removed and then re-inserted—along with those of the opposite sex—in an artificially constructed cavity in the lower abdomen. Its body violently rejected the treatment, causing a syndrome that closely resembled a type of cancer. No cure had been found and none was in sight. The organs were removed, but the condition of the patient continued to deteriorate.

"Nobody would tell me what was wrong with me. All my fantasies disappeared. My body went haywire. I simply fell apart. Finally, I got to see a doctor from outside the project. He said it would be a miracle if I lived six months. That was almost two months ago. Meanwhile, all the other ones died."

Marilyn had tears in her eyes. "That's horrible, I'm so sorry. What about the people who organized all this? Are they in jail?"

"Jail?" exclaimed Unity. "They practically run the planet. I'm talking about some of the most powerful people in CityTech. They hushed up the whole thing. I'm surprised my little friend left me alone with you. Maybe I shouldn't have told you anything. If they find out, you could be in trouble."

I could hardly be in more trouble, thought Marilyn. "But this is all wrong," she declared, sounding convincingly naïve. "Somebody has to be accountable for this. Can't you just go to the press?"

Unity chuckled. "Does it look like I can go *anywhere?* I can't even go to the bathroom by myself. And I'm constantly being watched."

"What if you could go? Would you do it?"

"In a second. But I think you've had one too many bunga nuts. Uh oh, here he comes." The surveillance was approaching, fifty yards and closing.

"So tell me more about your real estate career," said Melinda Pryce. "I'm thinking of acquiring some property. Maybe you can advise me."

Unity cracked a thin, wise smile. "Sure. But I'm a bit tired right now," it said, as the guard, face impassible, placed a pill on its tongue with one hand and poured water into the tiny mouth with the other. The two friends said their good-byes. The embracer was taken away.

The wheels in Marilyn's head began to turn. A kidnapping was clearly in order, but reinforcements were essential. How could it be pulled off? Just the act of contacting headquarters would be risky, not to mention the arrival of additional Root agents on the scene. But it had to be done. With possession of the embracer, they just might have the bargaining chip they needed to force Harris's hand.

The next morning, after breakfast, Marilyn went to the main office and asked to use their computer. It was an old model, but all she needed was to send a textual message. In her letter to headquarters, she used the latest scrambled code, reconstituted since the collapse of Operation Spearhead. After explaining the situation, she asked for a strike force to meet her at midnight at the intersection of the main highway and the private road leading to the R&R Retreat. The entire message was hidden within a letter to her "company," offering several ideas for product development and marketing. At the last minute, however, Marilyn was seized with doubt about the prudence of her action, and she scrapped the communiqué. Instead, she sent a message to the Root agent at Frendo, telling him that she would be there in two hours. Several code words indicated high priority.

Within ten minutes, Marilyn was back on the highway, retracing her steps. She made no stops along the way. Soon after her arrival, she and the other agent contacted Ingerman. She presented her proposal for the kidnapping of the embracer. Without hesitation, the chief approved the idea for that very night. The strike force would meet her at 2:15 AM at the end of the private road. Marilyn hopped back in her car, and returned to R&R Retreat in time for supper.

After a delicious *potage de plankton à la coastale* served in the R&R dining room, the psychologist once again walked down to the lakefront. Her new friend was there. She struck up a lively conversation about real estate, tapping into Unity's vast, albeit outdated, knowledge of the market. The guard announced that he was going to the bathroom. As soon as he was out of earshot, Marilyn wore her concerned look. "Oh, Unity, we've got to get you out of here."

"Keep dreaming. But if you know a way, you'd be my hero. I have nothing to lose. But there's not much I can do to help."

"I have an idea," she said. "Let's talk about it in the morning."

"Okay," said the embracer, with a look of friendly skepticism. "See you."

Marilyn returned to her cabin. At 1:30 AM, she departed on foot, heading down the winding private road. At several minutes past two, she arrived at the main highway. There was no sign of her comrades. She sat on a rock and breathed in the cool night air. Marilyn extracted every bit of tranquility she possibly could from the final moments before the operation, as this was most certainly the calm before the storm. She stiffened her resolve, clenching her teeth in defiance of the mighty TransTech world and all it represented.

Her serenity was brought to an abrupt end by the arrival of a dark blue van. The front window on the driver's side rolled down; she immediately recognized Reginald Burns. He motioned with his thumb to the empty seat beside him. She climbed in. In the back of the van were five men in black body suits, each armed with pistols. They advanced slowly down the road.

The plan, she soon learned, was to storm the cabin. They would eliminate the guard on the spot, putting his body in the van for disposal en route. Talking was forbidden during and after the taking of the cabin, until they rejoined the highway. Marilyn would count fifteen seconds after the others exited the van before she left the vehicle. She was tasked with getting to the embracer as fast as possible, and then exercising a calming influence. One agent would remain in the vehicle to provide cover. From the time the first person left the van—some forty yards from the cabin—until the time they rolled away, would take approximately one minute. Marilyn's car was to be left on site, so as not to attract attention by its absence.

Her heart was in her throat as they passed through the main compound, and then onto a tiny unpaved road leading to a cluster of cabins. They came to a halt within visual range of the target structure. One of the agents opened a briefcase containing a sensing device, which he aimed at the cabin. After turning a couple of dials, he nodded in the affirmative, and then showed the others a screen that indicated the vital signs of the two humans, as well as their position within the cabin. Both of them were asleep.

Silencers were placed on the pistols. The doors of the van opened, and the men jumped out. Marilyn started to count. The force broke through the cabin door and moved rapidly inside. By the time she passed through the doorway of the cabin, two agents were already lifting the guard's corpse off the bed. Burns waved her over to Unity, who was lying in a special crib, looking petrified. Marilyn put her face up close and smiled. Two men removed the crib and its inhabitant. Burns took the wheelchair, and Marilyn scrambled to collect whatever of Unity's clothing and medicine she could find, and then bolted for the van, which had already started to move. The others hoisted her into the back compartment. The two agents in charge of the guard were loading him into a body bag. Unity flashed a smile at Marilyn as it watched the proceedings.

After traveling about five miles along the main highway, they pulled over into a small clearing. Another van was waiting, with two men standing alongside. Burns and his five commandos changed into street clothes, shedding their weapons in the process. The two crews then switched vehicles, the Burns team leaving behind the cadaver, the weapons, the assault clothing, and related equipment. No words were spoken during the switch. In a matter of minutes they were back on the road in the other vehicle, the side of which was adorned with a large blue cross and the words "McKinney's Medical Transport."

Burns explained the itinerary. In approximately one hour and forty minutes they would arrive at the house of the Root agent at Frendo, from where they would cross the border separately and in a different manner. In the meantime, they would once again alter Marilyn's look, including a new hair style and color. The necessary equipment was already in the van. A passport had been prepared to match the makeover. They would try to cross the border without the assistance of the Root agent who worked as station supervisor, though he was waiting in the wings in case of complications.

As one of the men went to work on Marilyn's coiffure, she spoke to Unity, who seemed to be thoroughly enjoying the night's activities. She explained what was happening in very general terms.

Burns addressed the two of them, from the side of his mouth, as he continued to drive. "Don't relax yet," he cautioned. "We still have to smuggle Unity across the Line, and it needs to be smooth, with no suspicions aroused. We'll pose as a medical escort taking Unity to outerwart territory, to a special facility in the desert where the climate is more suitable for such patients. We have phony documents showing the transfer order."

"Good," said Marilyn. "We're ready."

"And by the way," added Burns, "sorry about that crack I made back in Jeptathia. I know you're good, and I'm glad you're with us right now."

At the Root agent's house in Frendo, the unlikely trio parted from the other agents and continued their trek in the medical van. They passed the border station without incident. Unity, presented to the officer on duty as a patient with terminal cancer, helped by moaning in feigned agony during the entire inspection. The officer, visibly disturbed, endeavored to complete the procedure as rapidly as possible.

Burns and Marilyn, both exhausted, took turns driving and sleeping for the three and a half hour trip to the Root command and training facility. Unity, for its part, was riveted by what it knew to be the last adventure of its life.

They came upon a small canyon, about two hundred yards wide and thirty deep. A brook ran down the middle, producing an oasis-like strip of vegetation. There was an old house, a barn, a corral, and several pens, none of them inhabited. It was the crack of dawn, and the silhouette of the buildings was visible against the steely-blue sky. The inconspicuous farmhouse contained highly advanced communications equipment and a fairly sizable armory. The hardened basement was encased in reinforced concrete, and had an emergency escape tunnel.

Ingerman was seated on the porch of the house, waiting to receive them. He was set to personally supervise the next phase of the operation. The commander approached the vehicle to greet his troops. They said their hellos and went into the house.

In a matter of minutes, they were seated around the breakfast table. "So this is the famous Unity," said Ingerman, flashing a big smile at the shriveled creature. "Marilyn told us a lot about you. I think she likes you." He laughed, and Marilyn blushed.

"We're getting along famously," said Unity. "Listen, I'm with you guys all the way. You could drop me as a human bomb out of a plane onto CloneFarm if you wanted to. It doesn't matter." Its face contracted in a display of anguish. "I won't be around much longer."

Marilyn bit her lip to avoid an unprofessional display of emotion.

The chief took command. "Unity, we're going to put you on the porch for a while. Marilyn and I need to discuss a few things. Burns will get you whatever you need." Breakfast ended, and the group split up.

The Root duo passed into the communications room, where they set themselves to the task of contacting Harris. He was given a simple ultimatum: Bring Forrester, alone and within eight hours, to a point in the desert close to their location—or they would inform the world about the embracer and its horrid tale. Certain details about Unity and its plight were included in order to erase any doubts concerning the veracity of the story.

"There it goes," said Ingerman as he dispatched the message. "Probably our last hope to ever see Forrester again."

CHAPTER NINE

▼

At that moment, Harris was seated in his office, putting the finishing touches on a status report for the Board meeting that evening. He was to present it himself in what figured to be a moment of glory. It was good news and more good news: The heliovision project was slightly ahead of schedule, and the success rate of tests run thus far had exceeded the norm by almost twenty percent.

Alongside this pinnacle of achievement came the news from the Root. Harris was shaken to the very depth of his being. The gamut of emotions associated with fear and frustration shot through his sinews like lightning, leaving him paralyzed in front of the computer. It took him a couple of minutes just to lift his arm, in order to wipe the sweat from his neck. Slowly, normal brain function returned, enabling the cyberengineer to calculate his reaction. There was no question: he must deliver Forrester. They had the goods; it was the perfect crime. Harris wondered how they could have pulled it off. There must have been a leak somewhere, as there was no publicity whatsoever regarding the "underachievers," not to speak of the location of the sole survivor of the ill-fated batch of embracers.

He needed a strategy, and fast. Should he go to Mr. J. and tell him what happened, or was it better to concoct a pretext for moving Forrester somewhere else? Should Bullock and Amrake be let in on the whole thing? There was no time for shuttle diplomacy. No, he concluded. Better to go straight to Mr. J. and seek his active cooperation.

Fifteen minutes later, Harris was seated in the conference area of Mr. J.'s office. Mr. J.'s face remained as stiff as marble during Harris's recitation of the bad news. With total calm, the security chief suggested that to save time, they immediately take his hypercush to the detention center. They would discuss the details en route.

During the ride, Mr. J. arranged for a jet to be waiting at the airport. He also spoke to three other people, snapping orders in security jargon, and then tapped some data into a mysterious panel on the dashboard. Harris was oblivious, having been overcome with anxiety. "Don't worry," said Mr. J., "we'll get you over there in time. The real problem is what to do when you arrive. For that, you're on your own."

Harris barely had the strength to nod his consent. Indeed, he thought, what would he do at that stage? He would have to improvise. There was simply no time to plan.

Mr. J. escorted Harris and Forrester to the air facility, and then loaded them into the waiting jet, which had a pilot and two security personnel on board. Mr. J. firmly shook Harris's hand, and wished him good luck. Forrester was placed in the cabin with the guards, while Harris sat in the cockpit, from where he could communicate with people at either end of the route. He looked at the pilot and shuddered. It was the same person that had brought him to CityTech for the first time. And, he soon learned, they were flying to the same facility near the BrainHost compound where the synchbox deal with Amrake had been concluded. Harris took a long sip of cephanil juice in an effort to suppress his growing sensation of terror over the entire turn of events.

As the jet lifted into the sky, Harris contacted Megan Bullock and told her that he was on his way to WestTech. There was a crisis connected to the heliovision project, and it threatened everything. He had to resolve it personally. He would explain everything when he returned. No need to alarm anyone; she could say, if necessary, that a rare opportunity arose to acquire some new technology. The boss was calm, reassuring her underling that there was no cause for concern; she would take care of everything. Harris was perplexed by the lack of controversy in the conversation. For that matter, he was puzzled by the ease with which Mr. J. had released Forrester. The unconditional cooperation on the part of the BrainHost top command seemed too good to be true.

The plane landed. The two travelers were escorted to their car, a classic all-terrain vehicle equipped with the navigation and communications equipment of a hypercush. Harris tapped into the navizoom the coordinates that had been sent to him by Ingerman and Marilyn.

The mood during the journey was grim. Neither of the two antagonists spoke. Harris felt humiliated. He resolved that once the incident was over, he would devote as much time and energy as possible to crushing the Root. Before, he had considered it to be an elaborate crime ring: deadly, but not a system-wide threat. But this was different. This had to be stopped. How exasperating could it get: A gang of blathering morons was going to scuttle one of the greatest scientific projects of all time? Okay, he thought, calming himself, the crisis would pass. Forrester slipped through their hands, but the surviving witness, the embracer, would be dead in short order. And in any case, once heliovision was an established reality, nothing could turn it back.

Less than an hour later, Harris brought the vehicle to a halt at the specified location. There was nothing to be seen but open desert. A message arrived on his datapad, indicating new coordinates for a spot to be reached on foot, some eight hundred yards away. Harris printed a diagram of the sector, and the two men began their solemn march into the wilderness.

After walking about two hundred yards, there was a huge explosion behind them. Harris and Forrester both reeled around to see the vehicle transformed into a ball of fire. Harris's spirit sank to a new low.

"Looks like someone doesn't like you," said Forrester, carrying a wide, ironic smile.

Harris did not absorb the words. He was watching his life burn up along with the car. Obviously, an explosive device had been planted in the vehicle—but would the Root have done it? There didn't seem to be a reason. After all, he would soon be their prisoner. Were CityTech people responsible? Was Mr. J. in on it? Bullock? Why would they do such a thing?

"Let's go," urged Forrester, softly pushing Harris's arm. "Now you'll meet my people. Believe me, they're more dependable than yours." He had to again nudge Harris, who had the demeanor of a zombie. They restarted their trek.

No words were spoken. Harris had to wait periodically for the limping, sweating, and huffing Forrester to catch up. Even for the younger and healthier cyberengineer, the mid afternoon desert sun was taxing. Harris wiped the sweat off his forehead and neck, looked back at the smoldering car in the distance, and thought that perhaps it would have been better if he were still in it.

They arrived at the edge of the canyon and peered into its interior. "So this is the world headquarters of the Root?" asked Harris, in a sarcastic tone.

"No," replied Forrester, happy to break the silence. "It's just a rest home for retired terrorists."

Harris's mouth displayed the beginnings of a smile.

From behind an outcrop emerged Ingerman, Marilyn, and two security officers. The officers frisked Harris. Marilyn darted straight to Forrester and threw herself into his arms. Ingerman patted him on the back, and then turned toward Harris. "Welcome," he said. Gesturing in the direction of the exploded vehicle, he added: "Looks like at the last service station they accidentally dropped some nitroglycerin into the tank."

Harris looked away.

"All right, let's go," said the chief, herding his minions down into the canyon.

When they entered the house, Harris was led to an old leather armchair replete with gashes and loose springs. The chief, Forrester, Marilyn, and Burns sat at close range. One of the security officers served cold beverages. Harris looked around the room. It was decorated with the shabbiest of used furniture. They economized on the frills, he surmised, in order to invest in critical items. He had noticed a sophisticated computer, a very expensive, state-of-the-art item.

Ingerman wasted no time. "We have something to show you," said the chief. Harris braced himself. A wheelchair rolled into the room, coming to a halt a yard from Harris's toes. The cyberengineer and the embracer stared at each other for what seemed like an interminable moment. Harris was devastated by the ghoulish spectacle. It was a scene from a nightmare; the bastard child catching up with the fleeing father. He was the defendant in the witness stand. He felt asphyxiated.

"Well," said Unity, in its high-pitched voice, "is this what you call a state of perfect happiness?" It looked at Harris with an expression of disgust, and then asked to be taken away.

Harris covered his face with trembling hands. His mind was a carrousel of self-flagellation, alternating between images of the embracer, the exploding car, Mr. J.'s reassurances, the Dome, and his bout of vomiting during the first coital matrix session with Templeton. The others nodded their agreement that the desired effect had occurred.

"I think it's time for you to rest," said Ingerman, as part of a preplanned strategy to let him stew in his own juices. "Mr. Burns, please show Harris to his quarters."

Harris complied, but was barely able to lift himself from the chair. Burns escorted him to a secured room in the basement that was to be under constant surveillance.

Unity asked to speak to Ingerman and the others. One of the officers wheeled it back into the main room. Visibly choked up from its encounter with Harris, it let its desire be known: "Aren't you going to punish that maniac?" it asked.

"Not right now," replied the chief. "That maniac—and I fully share your feeling—is the most valuable treasure our group has ever owned. He knows everybody who's anybody in CityTech, and is the world's leading expert in heliovision. His own people just tried to assassinate him." Ingerman leaned back and folded his arms.

"Which means," said Forrester, "that he just might help us. We need to work on him for a while. But he'll come around."

Unity looked disappointed and insulted. It turned its little shrunken head toward its best friend. "Marilyn, do you agree with them? Didn't you say they should all be in jail?"

Marilyn tilted her head down slightly as a pained expression crept over her face. "Well, he is in a sort of jail right now. Look," she said, in a voice filled with all of her feminine warmth, "our primary goal right now is to stop this horrible machine in its tracks, to make sure that what happened will never happen again."

The Root agents agreed upon an initial interrogation strategy: Harris would be left alone in his "jail" under close observation, until he literally begged to speak to someone. Then Forrester and Marilyn would probe his mind, seeking out the weak points. While waiting for Harris to arrive, Marilyn and Burns had amassed a small collection of audio-visual aids, including pictures of Harris's childhood neighborhood, before-and-after shots of Unity, and illustrations of the most bizarre and repulsive behavior in the coital matrix. Eventually, they figured, he would crack.

Forrester and Marilyn settled into their seats in the observation room, from where they could view and communicate with their subject. The room contained monitors that showed the interior of Harris's chamber from several angles. What they saw for the next eighteen hours could disturb even the most hardened operative. It was the portrait of a man losing his mind. At times, Harris would lie on the bed motionless, staring at the ceiling. At other times, he would run around the room, hurling himself against the walls while shrieking uncontrollably. Then he would curl up in a corner and sob. Finally, he screamed repeatedly, "Get me out of here! I want to go home!"

Forrester seized the opportunity, turning on the loudspeaker in the chamber. "Okay, no problem. But *where* is your home?"

Harris looked up at the area on the ceiling from where the voice originated, and then looked progressively more confused as he collapsed in a heap on the floor.

"Harris," said the voice of Forrester, "we know where your home is. We even have pictures of it to show you. When you're ready, of course."

He looked up with the face of a child who was just told that his broken toy had been fixed. "Yes," said the crushed figure of a man. "Yes, I do want to go home." He must have a home, he thought, everyone does. He tried to focus on his original home, in the more distant past, but he could not sustain a single image for more than a moment. The earliest abode he could picture with reasonable clarity was the seedy flat he rented when he first left the Academy. Was it possible, Harris thought with growing horror, that he had no home? Maybe there were other people who had no home. He remembered some words spoken at the Dome by one of the embracers: your home is really your state of mind, your spirit. A physical house in a fixed location is an impediment to spiritual fulfillment. It keeps humanity forever divided, yet another obstacle to attaining a perfect state of love among all people.

Another image crept into Harris's enervated mind's eye: his apartment in CityTech. Yes, that was it. That was his home! He pictured himself at the bar, preparing a hot swiffer, and then a cerebral plunge. Every cell in his body burned with a yearning for the comforts of Browser Beach, for his exquisite hypercush, his meteoric career, the office, the Dome, the Nice estate. But where was it? Why are they taking it away? And *who* is taking it away? It wasn't really the people at BrainHost; no, it can't be. Harris was in the fetal position, clutching the sides of his head.

He must get back. There's been a mistake, an oversight. He has to finish the job. So what if some embracers die, they knew the risks. Whenever a new medical technology is introduced, there are sacrifices to be made. Did no one die when heart transplants were first attempted? This is the same thing exactly. No one is happy about the suffering, but such sentimentality cannot be allowed to block a quantum leap in humanity's standard of living.

Harris jumped up, reinvigorated. He looked to one side and then another, his body assuming an aggressive posture. He pointed menacingly at the source of the sound. "Yes, I will go home," he shrieked. "You can't stop me. You're using the embracer to blackmail me. What do you want? Is it heliovision? Is that it, you want it for yourselves? Well you can't have it. It is what it is, it's an established fact." Harris burst out laughing from the obviousness of his words. He thought of where he was. These little peons are going to bring the whole CityTech machinery to a grinding halt? And do it by tricking him into feeling lonely and sentimental about some mysterious "home"? He put his hand on the wall to steady his body, which was being racked by laughter.

From sheer exhaustion, Harris soon found himself sitting on the floor, leaning against the wall. His neck and back were sticky from sweat, and a pungent odor emanated from his pores. It was the most intense outburst of emotion he had ever experienced.

Was it certain that Mr. J. engineered the car demolition? Far from it, reasoned Harris, as his normal powers of analysis began to return. This motley gang could easily have fired a missile at the car. They undertake far more complex operations. But who are they, these outerwarts who are ignorant of everything that drives the world, from heliovision to self-realization to cyberbiology to the sabbatical cradle to the latest trends in art and music?

"Harris," said the loudspeaker, "I want to come in and speak with you." Moments later, the door opened, and Forrester limped into the room. He sat down in the chair.

"So you're ready to go home," led off Forrester.

"Save the baby talk, doctor," retorted the defiant cyberengineer. "I'm over the initial shock. That stunt with the embracer was a good one, not to mention the car. You had me there for a minute."

Forrester, impassible, studied his prisoner. Harris certainly was bold; the audacity was real enough. But it was a superficial audacity, caused purely by environmental stimuli. Forrester conjectured that it was the deprivation of his usual pleasures that drove the man to his exaggerated devotion to CityTech. If Harris sensed that greater pleasure existed in Jeptathia, he would switch sides in an instant. The scene with Unity was merely a momentary stimulus that shattered the equilibrium of his nervous system. There was no underlying moral judgment involved. Remove the stimulus, and you remove the impact.

Harris decided to launch an offensive. The muscles in his face tightened. "You can't stop the march of civilization, my dear outerwart. CityTech leads the world, it sets the pace. And with good reason: We're on the verge of developments that would impress even you crackers out here in nowhere land." He paused to gauge the impact of his words. His interlocutor was looking him in the eye with a cold but attentive expression. Harris pressed on. "Dr. Forrester, tell me, what method do you use to copulate with your wife?"

Forrester, with great effort, stifled a laugh. It caused his neck and torso to convulse slightly, a movement that did not escape Harris's eye.

"So you think it's funny? Not surprising. Such is the reaction to be expected of you and your depraved people. You know you can't rise to the level of CityTech, so you mock it. You of course have no comprehension of people who don't want to have sex like animals, like dogs sniffing each other in the street. But don't worry, doctor, vast social changes eventually spread over the world's population. It's similar to eating with a fork and knife. At first, just a small number of people used these utensils, while the vast majority still ate with their hands. Then it caught on, to become the custom almost everywhere. So it will be with the coital matrix, and then heliovision." Harris's eyes widened with mention of the word. "Heliovision is a way of life, a transformation, the liberation of humanity."

Forrester let slip a look of disbelief. He needed time to regroup; he was feeling physically sick. At that moment, Marilyn asked Forrester via the loudspeaker if he could step out for a minute. He happily complied, leaving his prisoner alone in the chamber.

"I could see you were losing your patience," said Marilyn, as Forrester entered the observation room.

"I can't deny it. The personal insults I can brush off. But to gaze into his lifeless eyes and see the future of humanity, with no soul and no depth, is more than I can bear." He slumped into the chair.

Marilyn sat down beside him, and gently patted his forearm. "There's something I want you to see." She pressed some buttons next to the computer while Forrester watched Harris on the monitors. The cyberengineer was lying on the bed, immobile, face in a deadpan stare.

"Okay, it's ready," announced Marilyn, returning Forrester to the task at hand. She showed him a fresh item from the CityTech morning news: ROOT TERRORIST RING EXPOSED. Just under the headline was a picture of Harris, with the subheading "Inside job: CityTech cyberprodigy scuttles project and flees." Smaller pictures of Forrester and Marilyn appeared further down. Harris was portrayed as the ringleader. He was accused of selling trade secrets in order to gain entrance to BrainHost; sabotaging a major cyberbiological research effort (leading to the death of several program volunteers); and skipping town with his accomplices.

"These people may be Philistines," said Forrester, "but they're not stupid. They grabbed the opportunity to make the embracer affair public instead of waiting for the inevitable embarrassing leak."

"Should we show this to Harris?" asked Marilyn.

"Yes," he replied, in a somber tone of voice. "But first, let me grease the wheels." He hoisted himself from the chair and limped and huffed his way back to Harris's room. Forrester took a seat on the edge of the bed and looked at the deadpan countenance. Once again, he thought about the expressionless face, that it rarely displays a movement as the result of an internal spark, but only of a passing stimulus. And even then it is all or nothing, without subtlety.

Forrester, with a faintly ironic look, introduced the bombshell: "So, my dear cyberwart, why didn't you tell me that you were running a Root cell in CityTech?" Forrester interpreted Harris's motionless state as a sign of confusion. He then mimicked this state in his own posture, milking every ounce of advantage from the impact of his brazen revelation.

After several moments, Harris responded: "Is that your idea of a joke?"

"No, it's definitely not a joke. What would you do if I told you that your planetary elite just set you up to take the fall for the embracer affair?"

Harris swallowed hard. There was something about Forrester's manner of speaking that was utterly convincing. "You're bluffing," said Harris, his voice trembling.

"Am I?" replied Forrester, as he opened a side cabinet containing a computer. "Why don't you check some of the morning news reports in your beloved utopia?"

Harris moved the chair to the computer and accessed his preferred news sources. In a few moments he began viewing the bottomless pit of reporting generated by one of the most monumental scandals ever to hit CityTech. His body went limp.

"Excuse me a minute," said Forrester, leaving his prisoner alone to absorb the full blow.

He and Marilyn viewed Harris on the monitors. No words were needed to describe the macabre scene of a man literally watching his life unravel. Forrester stared intensely at the screens. "I think Ingerman needs to be in on this. I'll be right back. Take note of anything unusual." He headed upstairs into the house.

It was the last time Marilyn would ever see him. What transpired next was as unexpected as it was devastating. A high-pitched wail rose in volume to an ear-splitting crescendo, followed by a massive explosion in the house above. Despite the hardened basement, the direct hit loosened pieces of the ceiling, some of which fell around Marilyn. Other wails and explosions could be heard in the distance.

It took her several moments to gather her wits, finally realizing that she must exit the building immediately or face death. She grabbed her purse and headed for a nearby door that led to the escape tunnel. The corridor was filled with smoke and the air temperature was rising. As the young woman reached for the door, she hesitated: What about Harris, locked in the interrogation room? Having no time to debate the issue, her merciful nature carried the day, and she headed back down the hall to the little chamber.

Harris was still seated at the computer, in a state of non-comprehension. He failed to acknowledge Marilyn's presence.

"Come on," she pleaded, pulling the debilitated body with all her force. "We have to get out of here." She pushed and cajoled Harris into the corridor, and from there into the tunnel. They scurried through, arrived at the end, and climbed a ladder up to ground level. Marilyn waited for several minutes just below the hatch, in case the area was being scanned. She gingerly opened the hatch, and the two emerged from the ground.

The scene around them was appalling. The house was a smoldering ruin, and the other structures also were destroyed. It seemed that the site had been attacked from the air, and rather efficiently at that. Marilyn was horrified by the sight of the house, all too aware of the fate of its occupants. Her feelings of loss were somewhat muffled at that moment by the sensation that in all likelihood, she would soon be sharing the fate of her comrades.

She turned to Harris, who was sitting on the ground, gazing at the wreckage. "We have to go," she insisted.

"What for?" he replied. "We have no food, no water. We might as well wait here, until they come for us."

"I'm leaving," shrieked Marilyn, by now at her wit's end. "You can stay, I don't care. You can sit here all you want and stare at this place." She gestured in the direction of the carnage, arms flailing wildly. "Yes…look at it, your beloved citywarts just killed some of the nicest, most devoted people in the world." Tears were rolling down her cheeks. Harris, despite the preoccupation with his shattered life, experienced a fleeting inner movement of compassion for the distressed female.

Marilyn turned her back on the cyberwart and began walking away. She remembered that there used to be an old vehicle in the garage a few hundred yards down the creek; perhaps it was still there. She alternately walked and ran with a jerky motion, occasionally falling over a piece of debris. The smoke wafting across the area severely limited visibility.

Harris lingered for several moments, then sprang up and ran toward his sole hope for salvation. Marilyn did not look his way as he pulled up alongside. She was sobbing and mumbling to herself. "You and your matrix-vision, or whatever it is. That's it—no more warmth in the world, no more intimacy. Cruel, cold death. Yes, you're like death warmed over." She stopped dead in her tracks and turned toward Harris, pointing at him. "This is a man? You call yourself a man? Are you happy now?"

She continued her forced march, which by now led them down a narrow path along the creek, partially blocked by pricker bushes and other scrub. Harris followed close behind, not responding to his unlikely companion's tirade. His mind was enveloped in fear, confusion, and despair. He only half listened, instead concentrating on an escape strategy, which at the moment was looking rather bleak.

A glimmer of hope appeared when they came upon the garage, partially hidden within a small depression. Harris raised the sliding door, exposing the front end of an old-fashioned pickup truck, complete with rusted fender and cracked headlight. He climbed into the driver's seat, and turned the key that was waiting in the ignition. There was no response. Marilyn poked around the grill, found the latch, and opened the hood. The engine was covered with metallic dust. Her heart sank.

The two maintained their silent poses for several minutes. Harris eventually got out of the vehicle, moved slowly to the garage entrance, and surveyed the scene. It was almost night. The air was cool and still, with intermittent traces of smoke. He turned around and scanned the garage wall: There were assorted tools, a sink, some old gloves and rags, a gasoline can, several blankets, a first-aid kit, and some crackers and cans of food, perhaps enough to keep one person alive for a few days. He opened the faucet, releasing a weak but steady stream of water.

What would he do, stranded here with this outerwart female? Maybe, he thought, they would just sit there and await their bitter fate. There was no hope anyway; it was checkmate. Even if he managed somehow to leave the desert alive, which was by no means likely, the authorities would be looking high and low for him. His face probably was plastered over every computer in the TransTech world. What about trying to vanish into some obscure part of outerwart territory? No, he concluded, that's not a life. After everything he had experienced, to dwell among these people? There were simply no available options. Every course of action was doomed.

Harris's mounting frustration needed an outlet. "Who told you about the death of the embracers?" he exclaimed, looking directly at Marilyn.

"I can't tell you," she answered, with cool detachment. "I swore never to divulge his name."

"That little rat," responded Harris, clenching his teeth. "Beecely has hounded me since the Academy. I thought that in CityTech I'd be rid of that stinking wart." Marilyn's face expressed skepticism. Harris continued to vent. "I wasn't the only one at the Academy to suffer. We were research assistants, but he treated us like slaves. You had to do what he said, no matter what, or you'd feel it in your grade. A colleague and I complained, so he accused us of cheating. To add insult to injury, he posed as our protector, arguing for leniency before the faculty committee. The whole thing was humiliating. Later, when I was offered a two-bit job at InterFun—even though I knew Beecely was behind it—I grabbed it because it was all I could get."

Harris was pacing back and forth like a professor expounding upon a grand theory. "But that's not all. Let's talk about his escapades at CloneFarm. He jumped onto the embracer bandwagon in full force. Of course, others did the work and he took the credit. Until one day he decided to do a few things himself. By the time CityTech figured out what was going on, it was too late, the damage had been done. We had to close down the CloneFarm end of the project and bring everything back to CityTech. It was a mess." Harris stopped moving and sighed heavily. He slowly climbed onto the hood of the truck and rested his body, with his back to the windshield.

Marilyn weighed the explanation she had just heard. Perhaps there was some truth to it, she thought. Maybe Harris was not the ogre she had figured him to be. Still, the things they were doing to Unity, even before the CloneFarm mishap, were atrocious. "Don't you think," she ventured, "that some of the things you were doing, even according to the plan, were just a teeny bit weird? I mean, did you really think nothing would happen when you implanted female sexual organs into a man, and vice-versa?"

Harris's armor was dented. A fleeting hesitation darted across his mind. He quickly regained composure. "I admit it sounds strange. But you have to realize that we're talking about the cutting edge of scientific research."

"Oh, God," moaned Marilyn. She looked at him in disbelief. "I just don't get it. You lived through the Division. You saw what they did, you heard the lies. Our whole world was wiped out. Doesn't that mean anything to you?"

Harris was wearing what had become by now a permanent frown. "Can't you let the war ever die? Will you be reliving it forever? Sure, I saw what happened. But it was a war. You're conveniently forgetting what the other side did. What about the massacre at Pointed Bluff? That will go down in history as one of the cruelest and most hateful acts ever committed."

Marilyn shuddered. One of the outerwart platoons at Pointed Bluff was led by a young lieutenant named Reginald Burns. Burns, for his part, claimed that his men were fired upon, and that they simply unleashed a disproportionate retaliation against the *armed* civilian population. The incident was a great embarrassment for the outerwart world, and provided endless grist for the TransTech propaganda mill.

"You're not the only one to have suffered," continued Harris. "There were millions of us, and we rebuilt our lives. And was that so terrible? Did you have it so bad? You had healthy nourishment, a nice apartment, plenty of entertainment, a great career. In short, an entire culture designed solely for your own personal fulfillment." Harris now looked Marilyn in the eye. "And did anyone in CityTech ever force you to do anything?"

Marilyn looked away.

"You're just like my parents," said Harris. "They could have rebuilt their lives, but instead they sat around and sulked. Constantly complaining about the TransTech world. Well, in the end it killed them."

"What do you mean?" asked Marilyn, with softened eyes.

"They became more and more isolated, like hermits. In their final days, they never left the boarding house. They both died of aggravated neuronomies."

"That's awful," said Marilyn, in a barely audible voice.

After a few minutes of silence, she began to inspect the available rations. She opened the box of crackers, a can of peas, and a can of salted beef. Harris received his portion with a long face, but thanked her for making the effort. Few words were exchanged during the meal. After cleaning up, Marilyn fell asleep in the cab of the truck, while Harris used the blankets to construct a makeshift bed in the cargo area.

The next day, they did not leave the garage except to take care of their needs, for fear of being spotted from the air. They were both surprised that a force had not been dispatched to sweep the area on the ground. Perhaps, they conjectured, it was assumed by the authorities that everyone at the site was killed. Nevertheless, movement during the day still seemed risky.

Toward the late afternoon, Harris became edgy, and resumed his pacing. Marilyn was sitting on the floor, leaning against the side post of the garage door. Harris was beside himself with frustration over the dead end in which he had become trapped.

"You think I'm a monster, don't you?" he lashed out. "It's your whole damn attitude. From the first moment we spoke at the restaurant. Even when you tried to butter me up, it didn't work. I could see where you're coming from. You look at me, speak to me like I was a mutant from outer space." Harris was pacing vigorously. Marilyn sat up straight. She looked directly at him; their eyes locked momentarily before he broke the stare to continue his movement.

Truly moved by the honest and forthright tone of his eruption, she wanted to set the record straight. "Harris," she said gently but firmly, with a slight quiver. "I have nothing against you personally. But you have to understand—what you were doing simply could not continue. I'm talking about everything happening at CityTech: the embracers, the Dome, Nice, and the rest. It's the end of us all."

The cyberwart reacted by staring vacantly into the interior of the garage.

"Tell me something," continued Marilyn. "Do you remember our neighborhood before the Bombardments? Our high school? Do you remember *me*?"

Harris's face grew pale. He rarely thought about such subjects. The memories were murky and caused him great emotional pain. "I don't like to talk about it," he responded. "I don't remember much anyway."

"I have some nice memories from that time," recalled Marilyn. "Our high school was a lot of fun. Do you remember the principal, Mr. Bollen? What a nerd!"

Her amusement was greeted by a prolonged pout on Harris's face.

"Hey," she said, "can I ask you a personal question?"

"Go ahead," he replied, with a look of ennui. "It doesn't really matter anymore."

"Do you ever feel the need for affection, for tenderness, from a woman? To be held and comforted?"

Harris stared blankly into space. Marilyn was not sure whether he had heard the question, was deep in thought, or simply chose to ignore the query. But then he looked at her and responded. "I understand perfectly well the need of which you speak. At times I have felt it, yes. But I aspire to a higher state of being." He paused momentarily, and then continued, enunciating each word. "This tenderness is yet another form of exploitation, a way to selfishly use another person, to drain them of their capacity for self-realization. To a certain extent, we have no choice. What I mean is, under normal circumstances, we must satisfy our sexual impulse. But once this requirement is met, there is no excuse for forcing another person to be one's emotional garbage pail. It may seem to be beneficial for the aggressor, but in the end neither side really benefits."

Marilyn no longer was shocked by this line of reasoning, though she had grown weary of it. She opened up a new line of attack: "What about the way your friends at CityTech betrayed you? Doesn't that change the way you feel about the Dome, the embracer project, and all the rest?"

"It changes nothing," responded Harris, at a slightly higher volume. "First of all, it's not 'my friends'. All it takes is one person. I have to find out who did it and then clear my name. I think it was the BrainHost security chief. I never did like the looks of him."

Marilyn laughed under her breath.

"You think that's funny?" asked Harris, looking insulted.

"Oh, stop being so stiff," she retorted. "Of course your situation's not funny. What's funny is you."

"Me?"

"Yes, you. They could skin you alive and hang you up by your toenails in front of BrainHost, and you'd still be singing the praises of the coital matrix." She burst into a fit of giggling. "Coital matrix? That's what you call making love? You're so out of it."

Harris looked down, and in a low, barely-audible voice: "You understand nothing of my work."

This statement prompted yet another round of giggling. After several moments it subsided.

Nightfall was approaching. Marilyn stood up and announced that she was going down to the creek to bathe herself. When she returned half an hour later, she found Harris in the same spot. "So, what are you going to do now?" she asked, in a subdued tone of voice.

"I don't know. I guess I'll try to get back to civilization, and then contact someone in CityTech, someone I can trust." Harris displayed a distressed face, as one who was trying to convince himself of the veracity of his own words.

"You really think someone will talk to you?"

Looking grim, he stood up and stepped away several paces. After a long silence, he turned his head slightly and said over his shoulder: "I don't know. But I might as well try. There's nothing for me in outerwart territory. Nothing." He looked up at the stars that dotted the sky, and then returned to his perch on the hood of the pickup truck. "What about you?" he asked.

"I have to make contact with whoever's left in the high command," responded the Root agent. "That is, if there's anybody left." She sighed deeply as she opened the last of their provisions, a can of gelled pork. Harris viewed the emerging meal with a noticeable look of disgust. Marilyn continued: "If there's no group to go back to, I'll have to disappear for a while, maybe somewhere far away. I know a few people from the rank-and-file who could help me do it."

"You seem to be skillful at changing your identity," said Harris, lifting a lock of his hair to emphasize the point.

"So far it's worked," said Marilyn, as she served the heliovision expert a small plate of gelled pork and a glass of water. "Here you go, sir. Your order is ready."

Harris managed a tiny smile as he received the plate.

"We have no more food," said Marilyn. "We need to get somewhere. The closest town is about twenty-five miles away. We could make it if we take water." She paused for a moment. "Do you want to come with me? We could go separately if you prefer."

"I think we're stuck with each other," said Harris. A fleeting thought entered his mind, of performing the coital matrix with Marilyn. He instantly rejected the idea, surmising that she would mock the entire procedure and turn it into a farce. "Do you know how to get to this town?" he inquired.

"More or less," she replied. "We follow the main road in the opposite direction from where you came. It would be too risky to walk along the highway, but we can keep it in visual range, maintaining a distance of about five hundred yards."

Harris was beginning to respect the outerwart female, having witnessed several times her organizational acumen. "Should we leave right now?" he asked.

"No. It would be preferable to move at night, when it's cool. But I'm not sure enough about the terrain. So let's leave at the crack of dawn. I think if they wanted to sweep the area, they would have done it already, so we can chance it. By the way, we need to wash out that gasoline can and fill it with drinking water."

Harris volunteered for the task and carried it out with a high degree of efficiency. The young woman watched, noting that Harris was slim and strong, and quite masculine in his body movement. If he would just warm up a bit, she thought, he actually would be attractive.

He turned the can upside down to let it drain, and then announced that he also needed to go down to the creek to bathe, in advance of his reinsertion into human society. He was finding his own body odor to be oppressive.

He made his way down the trail, slowly traversing the hundred and fifty yards or so of scrubby terrain. A sliver of moonlight assisted his vision. At the water's edge, he disrobed. His toes froze as he gingerly advanced into the stream. He listened to the nocturnal sounds of the desert. The usual buzzing of insects was joined by a vague droning sound in the distance. It became more intense, and then there was a massive explosion. The garage where Harris had been only moments before was transformed into a crater. A large ball of fire rose up from the site.

He grabbed his clothes and waded as fast as he could to the other side of the creek. Once across, he hastily dressed himself and bolted for the far edge of the canyon. As he ran, it occurred to him that his action was futile. Would he outrun the security forces, in an unknown desert, with no food or water? Perhaps he should just stop and await his fate. But some vestige of a survival instinct propelled him forward. And his powers of reason told him that he must exploit the night to move as far as possible. During the day he would be paralyzed from the heat.

Harris ascended from the canyon, and began his trek across the flat, open desert. He moved in the general direction that Marilyn had indicated. His thoughts wandered to the outerwart female. He briefly considered her death, and even experienced some regret. The sensation quickly passed, however, as he refocused on the current, rather precarious situation.

About an hour later, he came upon an old, rusted barbed-wire fence, of the coiled concertina variety. A sign on the fence read DANGER: MILITARY PRACTICE AREA. KEEP OUT. He followed the fence for several minutes until an opening appeared, and then climbed through with little effort.

The terrain began to change. The ground was somewhat hilly and more rocky. He came across some traces of military practice: expended bullet casings and artillery shells. Harris's body was cold and his throat parched from thirst. He happened upon an abandoned jeep, and searched through it for water. There was an old canteen, but it was putrid. He looked around in desperation. He decided to make a sweep of the area; perhaps there were other options. He ascended a nearby hill. The terrain in all directions had a pallid, steely gray tone that compounded the morose feeling in his heart. There was an extra-terrestrial air about the scene. It was a geologist's paradise, with multiple varieties and sizes of rocks strewn helter-skelter upon a perfectly hard and smooth floor.

Harris faced the specter of his private Gehenna. His body was one sordid ache of thirst, exhaustion, and despair. He could survive for a few more hours at best. Even so, it was only a matter of time before the sector would be surveyed, at which time he would be transformed into a cloud of dust. There was no escape.

His legs were like two lead pillars as he ambled down the slope. He dragged himself toward the jeep, frequently losing his footing among the haphazard array of rocks. A fall left his upper arm bruised, but he felt strangely satisfied, as if for a moment the pain had brought him back to a real existence.

Harris began to experience the first symptoms of delirium, walking a tightrope between reality and oblivion. His thoughts became disassembled and violently rearranged, like fragments of a house spinning inside a tornado.

As his body sagged onto the rusty fender of the army vehicle, the atmosphere weighed on his face with its parched, chalky consistency. His lower lip cracked and he tasted a mixture of blood and dust. He climbed into the front seat and collapsed, letting his arms hang down along the sides of the seat. The index finger of his left hand came into contact with a piece of plastic that had escaped his earlier search. He stood up, lifted the seat, and beheld a black jerrican. He hoisted the largely depleted container and opened the cap, but his nostrils were greeted by an odor of mildew and stagnation. He drank the water, despite his profound disgust.

Harris climbed back into the seat and slumped forward, resting his cheek on the steering wheel. He remembered that BrainHost's first release of heliovision was scheduled for that very day. Nothing can stop it now, he thought. Too bad he would not be there to see it.

He spent the next two hours suspended between reality and dream. He was barely aware that the sun was rising. A droning noise filled his ears. What a way to go, he thought. At least it would be quick.

CHAPTER TEN

▼

The drone became more pronounced, but it was different than the one that preceded the attacks on the house and the garage. Harris looked up. An immense helicopter descended from the heavens, and then hovered about fifty yards above his head. The entire area was bathed in a blinding light. A voice on a loudspeaker said, "Harris, don't be afraid. We're going to rescue you."

Why don't they just get it over with, he thought.

The helicopter landed, sending a whirlpool of dirt across Harris's face. It was a scene from a science-fiction movie. Steps slid out of the giant metal insect, and out came none other than William Nice III, in the flesh. Dressed in his black robe, he approached the cyberengineer. "Thank goodness you're alive," he said, shouting to overcome the noise of the engines. "We thought it was too late. Come on, let's go." He put his arm around the shell-shocked fugitive and escorted him into the helicopter.

The back of the aircraft contained a small luxury apartment. Nice guided Harris onto a simple plastic chair, explaining that in a few moments he could take a shower and then relax on one of the sofas. Seeing the look of shock and disbelief on Harris's face, Nice reassured him. "Don't worry, it's for real. I'm on your side. I'll explain everything in a few minutes."

From the galley emerged Alexandra Humboldt-Weizmann, carrying a tray with a pitcher of ice tea and some cookies. "This is just to get you refreshed. We'll have a meal after you clean up."

Harris greedily drank the contents of the pitcher and settled back in the chair. The helicopter was already in the air and heading to CityTech. Nice showed the exhausted ex-fugitive to the bathroom, where he took a long, exquisite hot shower. A change of clothes was waiting as he stepped out.

The three associates relaxed in the lounge as they munched on hors d'oeuvres. Harris wanted to sleep, but was tense with curiosity to hear the story. Nice reported that it took him a day or two to figure out what was transpiring. From the outset, he didn't believe the disinformation being spread by Megan Bullock. He lacked the ammunition needed to confront her directly, so he engineered a quick investigation. He first spoke to Mr. J., who told him that he did indeed take Harris and the outerwart surgeon across the Line. Mr. J. grudgingly divulged their whereabouts. When Nice tried to fly into the sector, he was prevented from doing so by the TransTech security forces. It took even more time to sort through that mess, only to find out that again, Bullock was behind it. Nice pulled a few of his own formidable strings to call a halt to the manhunt. The new policy was implemented just after the attack on the garage. Fortunately, the pilot of the attack aircraft neglected to return and strafe the area, overconfident after his direct hit.

"We were lucky," added Humboldt-Weizmann. "You and that outerwart woman made it out of there just in time."

"You mean I made it out," said Harris. "Just by chance, I had gone down to the stream to wash up. But she stayed in the garage."

"No she didn't," said Nice. "We did a full groundscan of the blast area. If she had been there, her remains would have shown up. Unless something happened to her since then, she's still alive."

Harris suppressed an initial reaction of satisfaction at hearing the news. Disappointed with himself, he declared emphatically: "So she slipped through our hands again."

"We'll get her, don't worry," said Nice. "But more importantly, we've got to get *you* back on track. When we arrive, I'm bringing you to my estate for a press conference. I'm going to explain the horrible mistake that has occurred. Also, that Bullock was arrested, Mr. J. was suspended pending an investigation of his actions, and that your colleague here is going to be the new CEO of BrainHost."

"Couldn't be a better choice," said Harris, exchanging a smile with Humboldt-Weizmann.

"Another choice will also be announced," said the new CEO. "That you, my dear cyberwart, are going to be in charge of all research and development. No more fooling around. We've got to get things re-established as quickly as possible."

After they dined, Harris reclined his worn body on the plush sofa. He sank deeper and deeper into a luscious sleep. He dreamed that he was bathing in the creek, and that Marilyn was standing on a ledge above him, giggling at the sight of his nakedness. When he opened his eyes, he saw Humboldt-Weizmann's wooden features leaning over him.

"I was just about to wake you. You really slept! Anyway, we're here."

Harris hoisted himself and glanced out the window. They had landed in the yard next to the mansion on the Nice estate. Off in the distance was the Dome of Ascent, looking particularly luminous in the midday sun. Nice strolled in from the cockpit, with a satisfied air about him. "Let's do it," he declared. "Press conference in Amphidrome 6 in twenty minutes."

As the threesome stepped off the helicopter's stairway, they were met by several security personnel, and by Nice's personal media adviser. The group entered the main hall and headed for Amphidrome 6. It was the same spot where, during the picnic, Harris had seen the dive-bombing extravaganza. Currently, the space resembled a plain, empty theater, and it looked much smaller than it did back then.

There was already a throng of reporters and a smattering of VIPs. Nice motioned to his two underlings to sit at the table that was set up on the stage. Behind them, at the back of the stage, was the standard BrainHost hexaflash presentation, repeating itself every twenty-three seconds. As Harris approached, he was intercepted by Amrake.

"Harris, my boy," he beamed as they shook hands. "I'm so glad the truth is out. I told you that you were one of us, remember?"

Harris nodded his agreement but maintained a restrained demeanor. There were too many unanswered questions regarding Amrake's conduct during the entire affair.

Nice kicked off the press conference with his customary punctuality. With grave voice, he explained that a "horrible travesty" had occurred. Harris had remained loyal throughout the episode, even risking his life to escape Root captivity. No, it was Bullock who was behind it. Nice played a short tape of the former CEO confessing to everything: framing Harris, causing the damage to the embracer project, attempting to cover it up, and more. Harris wondered how Nice had extracted such a broad confession, covering even acts for which Bullock obviously was not responsible. He glanced at Humboldt-Weizmann, who was seated next to him. She tightened her mouth, as if to say, "stay quiet." Harris turned away and adopted a deadpan stare.

Nice confirmed that the commander-in-chief of the Root was killed, along with top agent Ebenezer Forrester and other personnel, while another key operative was still at large. He went on to announce the reshuffling of the BrainHost leadership. He asked Harris to stand up. The cyberengineer was treated to a round of roaring applause. Harris's comeback was broadcast live to every corner of the TransTech world.

When the event was over, Nice approached Harris. "You need to go home and get some rest. But would you mind joining me first for a few minutes in private?" Without waiting for an answer, he led the new head of R&D over to the main bar. Security personnel and other members of the entourage took up position just out of earshot. The two collaborators sat on elegant armchairs that had once been the property of Queen Victoria.

"Harris, I'm glad you're back."

Harris cracked a modest smile as he looked at the prophet of the Dome. Every segment of Nice's visible skin had been perfectly flattened. His white hair looked like it had been subjected to an equivalent treatment. Harris noticed that when Nice spoke, he always looked directly at his interlocutor, yet the exact location of his focus was impossible to gauge with any certainty. It was always just a degree off from where one expected it to be. Moreover, the left eye was always open wider than the right. Harris had been distracted by it ever since their first conversation.

"I was always very impressed with you," said Nice. "I believe in you, Harris. A lot of people I deal with around here just go through the motions. But you're enthusiastic, you really move things around. That's why I know we can work together."

"Oh, I'm sure we can."

"I do hope you'll be joining me regularly at the Dome. Just come when you want, don't stand on formality. Anyway, I could use someone dependable around here. I can't always do everything myself, if you know what I mean."

Harris pledged that he would attend regularly, and that Nice could always count on him to do his best.

Half an hour later, Harris stepped across the threshold of his apartment. After a brief tour, he noticed that everything was intact, but that many items had been moved from their usual location. Apparently, the authorities had searched the flat, and then attempted to restore it to its previous state. He parked himself at the bar, and wired up a double cerebral plunge. His nerves thawed like ice cubes dropped into hot tea. As he surveyed his abode, he recalled his tirade against Forrester, when he had insisted that he knew where his home was. Now, he was absolutely sure. He was indeed home, and with a vengeance. The satisfaction that imbued his spirit was immense.

In the morning, Harris returned to the office. Helmutsen greeted him at the southwest port, just like on his very first day at BrainHost. But this time, instead of cold, suspicious stares, he was greeted everywhere with bubbling excitement. People he had never seen before wanted to shake his hand and congratulate him. It was a hero's welcome. His office was covered with flowers, gifts, and a pile of handwritten cards and letters. Helmutsen informed him that the CEO wanted to see him at his earliest convenience.

Harris went immediately. It was clear from the outset that Humboldt-Weizmann, as CEO, had adopted a more formal tone. He hoped that he could find a way to make her decompress, to return to the pleasant rapport of old. In any case, what she said was positive enough. She lauded Harris's work and extolled their joint future at BrainHost, sounding a bit like Nice. "So," she summarized, "I guess we'll both get back to work."

"Of course. But just one thing I wanted to ask about..."

"Bullock?"

"Yes."

"Harris, some things are better left unsaid. I'm sorry." She rotated toward her computer. He was a bit perturbed, but then figured he could reopen the discussion at a more opportune moment.

Over the next few days, Harris reintegrated into BrainHost life. It was an arduous but satisfying task. He worked nonstop, morning to night, and often well into the night. Heliovision was scheduled to be released in its final version in a matter of weeks. Moreover, he now had additional responsibilities by virtue of his promotion to head of all research and development.

Despite his dense schedule, he did not neglect his duties at the Dome. Nice could not have been anything but pleased with his progress. Harris was a model participant, and was soon helping new initiates get started. Nice was planning to let him officiate during a portion of the service, it was just a matter of choosing the right time. In addition, the two discussed ways in which heliovision could be integrated into the proceedings. This was also a question of timing. Too early, and there might be accidents, with repercussions for the reputation of the Dome. Too late, and a glorious opportunity might be missed.

One morning, Amrake was in Harris's office to sort out some paperwork. It was time, thought Harris, to discover the truth about the role of Bullock—and Amrake—in the grand betrayal. Judging by Humboldt-Weizmann's hushing up of the affair, he knew that to question anyone would be a risky proposition. But he could not imagine the continuation of his career at BrainHost without clearing the air and knowing the facts of the case. To begin with, what precisely did Bullock do, and what was her motivation? Why did she confess to deeds that were not of her doing? How did Nice extract the confession, and did he have his own account to settle with Bullock?

Amrake was gazing distractedly at the computer. It was the first time Harris had seen him pensive, without his usual bubbly enthusiasm and absolute concentration. Something had gone awry. Certainly, one could well understand: Amrake's mentor, one of the great idols of the TransTech world, was in prison, disgraced and stripped of her medals, as it were. But was that enough to cause his condition, thought Harris, or was he hiding something, fearful that someone would find out?

"Jason, I want to ask you something. But before I do, let me say that I have great respect for you, and I appreciate all you've done for me since the moment we met in Jeptathia."

Amrake looked upward from the monitor with a pained smile. "Thanks, Harris. So what is it you want to know?" He asked the question in a fabricated sing-song, not able to conceal his dread.

"I've been wondering what really happened with Bullock. Why did she do it? Was she just using me as a convenient scapegoat, or was there something else going on?"

Amrake sat up straight, seeming to regain some of his usual composure. "I think it was just that she was trying to save the company. Don't get me wrong, old boy, there's no justification for what she did. But don't take it personally. She would've done the same thing to anyone in your situation. It was just too convenient and too tempting."

Harris was skeptical of this version of events, but he wasn't sure why.

"If you want to know the truth," said Amrake, his arms outstretched in a gesture of appeal, "I told her not to do it."

A silence established itself for several moments.

"Anyway," he continued, "I'm finished here. Your pal Humboldt-Weizmann hates my guts, she always has. She won't kick me out the door, but it's clear enough that I'm not welcome." Harris refrained from further questioning, satisfied with the progress made thus far. Amrake had broken a taboo—his reluctance to discuss personal matters—and Harris assumed that more information would be forthcoming at their next chat.

Two weeks later, he was sitting at his desk after lunch, quietly munching some bunga nuts and perusing the day's news. A particular item caught his eye: ROOT TERRORIST NAILED. Marilyn had been arrested as she stepped off a ferry, somewhere on the other side of the planet. According to the report, she was traveling with false papers, posing as a refugee from a natural disaster. The boat was packed with thousands of people who had lost their homes in a devastating earthquake, and she was pretending to be one of them. Harris chuckled under his breath. That was clever, he thought.

The following week, after wrapping up a session at the Dome, Nice invited Harris for a drink at the main bar in the mansion.

"I appreciate your extra effort today. I really do."

"My pleasure."

"Listen," said the Dome leader, with a heavy voice. "I want to share some important news with you."

"Go ahead," said Harris, resting his hot swiffer on the table.

"The Root woman, Marilyn Sommers, you saw that they found her?"

"Yes."

"Well, she's here, in CityTech, at our detention center. What I'm about to tell you is strictly confidential."

"Of course."

"The news reports say that she's being held temporarily by the local authorities out there, where the boat was docked. But I arranged to have her brought here quietly. I did it because I have an idea."

Harris's curiosity was at its peak.

"I want to use her to break what's left of the Root; or, more accurately, to convince any remnants or potential sympathizers that the game is over, that all hope is lost." The former construction magnate was looking intensely at Harris. The discrepancy in the aperture of the two eyes was more pronounced than ever. "I have a little plan: We're going to arrange for our outerwart friend to become an embracer."

"An embracer?" exclaimed Harris, rather loudly, forgetting himself for an instant.

"That's right," replied Nice, calmly. "She knows that she'll get the death penalty for what she did, so there's an outside chance that she'll go for it. I doubt it, though. She's from the real hard core of the Root. It's simpler if she cooperates, but even if she doesn't, we can go to work on her."

Harris was horrified. "You mean, force her to become an embracer? But we never force anyone to do anything. You said that yourself at the Dome."

Nice remained placid, telling himself that Harris's outburst was a typical reaction of the naïve, enthusiastic personality type. These people can't make a move, he thought, without being convinced that they're going to save humanity. As annoying as it is, they are extremely useful. Thus it was prudent to avoid saying anything that could tarnish Nice's credibility in Harris's eyes.

"You're absolutely right," maneuvered the Dome prophet. "I guess I went overboard thinking about the enormous benefit for all of humanity. Can you imagine, Harris, the reaction of young outerwarts when they see that the most elusive Root spy of all time just *understood?* Not to mention the reinforcement of the folks right here in CityTech. It would be a massive springboard for our cause."

Harris was in turmoil. On the one hand, he did agree that the overall benefit would be substantial. But he could not avoid a fleeting image in his mind of Marilyn screaming as they strapped her to the operating table.

Nice could easily read the agony on Harris's face. "Listen," he said in his gentle Dome voice. "I know you don't want to hurt anyone. But in the end, it's better for her as well. I think you'd prefer this option to the death penalty. It's mandatory for Root terrorists, as you know." Nice paused, and then smiled. "Why don't we go visit her. You can convince her to do it. Wouldn't that be the best thing?"

Harris didn't see how he could possibly carry out such an assignment, but he agreed, so as not to further antagonize his mentor, and to buy some time as well.

"What are we waiting for?" asked a satisfied Nice. He summoned one of his assistants to arrange for a hypercush. In a matter of minutes, Harris once again found himself at the BrainHost detention center. Nice headed for the observation gallery, asking Harris to wait in the interrogation room.

He entered the room, and stood behind the same table where he had made his unsuccessful appeal to Forrester. Less than a minute later, the door opened, and a handcuffed young woman was escorted in by a guard. Harris did a double take: her hair was jet black and frizzy. Her skin was sunburned and chapped; her hands blistered and red. The eyes betrayed a terrible fatigue. Marilyn looked like she had lived through a war. He was struck by a fleeting impulse to touch her.

A long silence ensued. Harris sat down, indicating to the prisoner to do the same. Marilyn managed a tiny smile, and said: "Well, here we are again."

"Yes," said Harris, tensing his lips. "I thought you were blown up in the garage."

"I would have, had it not been for a fluke. Just after you left to go to the stream, I remembered I had some soap in my purse. So I started after you. I had gone about fifty yards when the missile hit. The force of the explosion threw me to the ground, but I wasn't injured."

Harris noticed Marilyn's nicely rounded breasts, and thought that they probably looked better just hanging there, than in a plasticase.

The Root agent continued her tale. "After the blast, I ran toward the main road. I followed it from a distance, just as we were planning to do. But after a while I was cold and hungry, so I descended to the highway and hitched a ride with a tractor-trailer. The driver was friendly, and treated me to a meal at a truck stop. There, I contacted a local Root sympathizer, who came to fetch me."

Harris was hanging on every word.

"The Root sympathizer and his wife hid me in their house for a few days. They arranged for me to be transported back to the border crossing at Frendo. With great difficulty, I contacted the Root agent there, who was keeping a very low profile. He had the equipment needed to manufacture a false passport, and he made one for me. I purchased a plane ticket for overseas, and flew out of the local airport. When I reached my destination, I heard about the earthquake, and came up with the idea of joining the refugees. Unfortunately, there was a TransTech security agent at the port, and he spotted me." Marilyn paused, staring dreamily at the wall of the interrogation room. "Do you think our personal fate is preordained?" she asked.

Harris was unable to formulate a response, feeling a paralysis creep over his anatomy. He looked at Marilyn and pondered her fate. She sensed that something was awry, but remained silent. He excused himself, and exited the room.

"What's the matter?" asked Nice, as Harris joined him in the gallery.

"I'm not sure. I mean, I don't know how to do it," stammered the cyberengineer. "I'm tired, I need to think. Can we do this tomorrow?"

"No problem," said Nice, barely managing to conceal his impatience. "Why don't you sleep on it. Come to the estate tomorrow after work. Everything will be just fine."

Harris thanked Nice profusely, took leave, and returned home. For the remainder of the evening, he was extremely agitated. He turned the situation over and over in his mind, analyzing it from every conceivable angle, but to no avail. Out of desperation, he wired up a double cerebral plunge and took a sleeping pill. Ten minutes later, he was snoring.

But he had a nightmare, dreaming that he was chaining Forrester to a table, while Nice, carving knife in hand, prepared to turn him into an embracer. As the knife came down, Harris realized that he was in a dream. He experienced a long and powerful sensation of falling. After a struggle, he forced himself into consciousness. He sat up in bed, body drenched in sweat.

He looked at the clock. It was 2:17 AM. He put on his bathrobe, went to the bar, and fixed himself a swiffer freeze. The shock of the nightmare wore off, but his equally dismal situation re-entered his mind, pushing all else aside. He could not see an exit from the maze. There was no way that he could "convince" Marilyn to become an embracer. It was simply not going to happen. But if he didn't, she would be executed, or worse, Nice would force her into it—by using drugs, torture, or blackmail.

There also was no way, thought Harris, that he could go to Nice and plead her case. The man could not be swayed. The very reason for his possession of the prisoner was to engineer a coup of this type, and he certainly didn't have any pity for her. In any case, arguing on her behalf would discredit him in Nice's eyes. In the end it would be counterproductive.

Harris tried to toughen himself: What is all this sentimentality? Why is he so concerned about Marilyn? Isn't she a spy—worse, a traitor—who would like nothing better than to see his life's work sent to the junkyard? What's the problem, he asked himself, just present her with the ultimatum, she'll refuse, and then turn it over to Nice.

He sat back, hoping that the solution would stick. But a knot of tension formed in his chest. There was no getting around the most vexing aspect of the entire predicament: *he cared about Marilyn.*

There was no one to whom Harris could appeal for advice. When he thought about it, there was nobody in CityTech he could trust, at least not at this level. The only remote possibility would have been Humboldt-Weizmann, but she was crossed off the list following her strange reaction to the Bullock affair.

He rehashed the various arguments until it was almost time to go to work. Finally, he became inspired: Yes, he would do what he had to do. His greatest test of all had arrived. If ever there was a time to repress all sentimentality, this was it.

Over the course of the day, Harris galvanized his resolve. He was so confident that he contacted Nice just after lunch and asked whether they could rendezvous immediately at the detention center.

After the two shook hands at the entrance to the jail, Harris assured his spiritual mentor that he felt much better and would fight tooth and nail to convince the Root spy to become an embracer. Nice breathed a sigh of relief. The two cohorts hurried to their respective posts.

Harris once again found himself across the table from the young woman. She looked happy to see him. "Marilyn," he began.

The Root agent was dumbfounded, as Harris had never before addressed her by name. "Marilyn," he said again, his eyes humid. "Do you trust me?"

"Yes, Harris, I do."

A tear rolled down his cheek. "If I told you to do something right now, would you do it, without hesitation?"

"Yes, Harris."

"And would you do it immediately?"

"Yes."

His face was wet and trembling. "Lean forward as far as you can." She complied.

"When you see what I do, you do exactly the same thing." He reached into his pocket, removed a small metal box, placed it on the table, and opened it. He kissed Marilyn on the forehead, took a pill from the box, put it in his mouth, and swallowed it.

"No!" shouted Nice, jumping out of his chair and bolting for the door. By the time he reached the interrogation room, Harris and Marilyn had passed into the next world.